DRAGONS
IN THE CLOUDS

David Blair

ARPress
ILLUMINATING IDEAS
EMPOWERING VOICES

Copyright © 2020 by David Blair

ARPress
45 Dan Road Suite 36
Canton MA 02021

Hotline: 1(800) 220-7660
Fax: 1(855) 752-6001

Ordering Information:
Quantity Sales. Special discounts are available on quantity purchases by corporations, associations, and others. For details, contact the publisher at the address above.

Printed in the United States of America.

ISBN-13   Paperback   979-8-89389-565-0
               eBook   979-8-89389-566-7

Library of Congress Control Number: 2024920622

DEDICATION

I would like to thank Lucy Palacios for always supporting my writing,
Bruno Gonzales for constant inspiration.
My son, David James Blair, for never doubting my talent.
And to all the inspiring writers/storytellers.
We can do this.

It simply isn't
an adventure
worth telling
if there aren't
any dragons.

by J. R. R. TOLKIEN

Imagination is more important
than knowledge.
Knowledge is limited.
Imagination encircles the World

—Albert Einstein

ACKNOWLEDGMENT

Tom Walsh- thank you for showing me the formula of storytelling. Without it, Dragons in the Clouds would be a blank page.

David T. Saint Albans – thank you for editing and character development. You took it up a notch.

Brenda Sonjag – Thank you for editing expertise.
Tammy Koelling – Thank you for taking "Dragons in the Clouds" to the world.

FOREWORD

Remember when you were young, being stuck inside because it was raining heavily outside. You and your siblings would be in your room, staring out the window watching the raindrops gathering into puddles. The thunder in the distance would be getting louder, and you knew it was coming your way. You and your brother or sister would run out to the living room so you could get a better view when the lightning started. But the real reason you ran out to the living room is because that was where your parents were. What you really wanted was the security of your parents being in the same room… But! What if I told you, you had every reason to be scared? What if I told you that lightning really is fire being blown from a Dragons mouth and that thunder is a Dragons roar! Dragons in the Clouds will reveal all that has been kept secret from you.

TABLE OF CONTENTS

INTRODUCTION
"DRAGONS IN THE CLOUDS"

In the Albion forest in the depth of night, a full moon illuminated the passing clouds. As the Moonlight Pierces through the pine trees. The forest gives off a creepy feeling, but three gallant knights were moving cautiously through it. They were royal knights serving the kingdom of Albion, led by Sir Jonathan.

As they navigated their way through the dense forest dressed in full armor, the moon overhead illuminated their path, creating the illusion that their well- polished armor was embedded with sparkling shiny twinkling stars in the dark night. Suddenly, a deafening sound shattered the dense, still forest, sending chills down the spines of Sir Jonathan and his companions. Fright was written on their faces.

Sir Jonathan screams, as a silhouette of an enormous beast struck from the sky and lifted him into the air. Its razor-sharp teeth firmly held its prey while taking flight with its huge wings. The beast flew in front of the full moon, revealing a perfect outline of a dragon and then vanished into the darkness of the starry sky. The two remaining royal knights screamed in horror as they scrambled to light their torches. With looks of pure fright in their eyes, they stood back to back with their swords drawn.

Chapter 1
Present Day

In the suburb of a modern city, it's a typical, Norman Rockwell evening. A yuppie named Ray Evans is coming home from an overseas business trip. Breathing a sigh of relief, he turned onto his street and saw a welcome sight, the home he has been away from for too long. A few seconds later, he slowed the car and pulled into the driveway of his house.

Ray parked and wearily emerged from the car only to hear the sweet sound of his little girl approaching.

"Daddy, Daddy!" exclaimed the pretty blonde-haired girl as she ran toward her father. "I missed you so much, Daddy!" Reilly, as she is called, is only eight years of age and full of energy as she jumps into her father's outstretched arms.

"Hey baby girl!" responds Ray, beaming with pride and joy as he holds his daughter tightly. "I missed you too, princess! And I brought you something!" Mr. Evans reached behind his back, pulled out the hidden present and gave it to his daughter. All smiles, he watched eagerly as Reilly unwrapped the gift: a toy dragon with a tiny opal ball in one talon.

"Oh Daddy, you know how much I love dragons," Reilly said, as she hugged her new toy. "Thank you so much, Daddy."

"You are welcome, sweetheart," he replied warmly. "Hey, you know what? That is not just any dragon; the old man who ran the gift shop told me it's a special dragon," added the father.

"What do you mean?" Reilly asked.

"During my trip to Europe, when I was in London, I went for a walk to buy you and mommy some gifts. I went past this old funny London shop and saw this little guy in the window, so, I went into the store. Of course, I knew you had to have it, so I asked the man how much it cost… and guess what?

The old man said it wasn't for sale. So, I asked him why he was showing it if it wasn't for sale. And then he told me a story about how this was the most courageous little dragon he had ever known."

Reilly interrupted her father, "What did he mean Daddy, does he know a lot of dragons?"

"Yeah baby, as a matter of fact, he said he did," replied her father, as little Reilly started to giggle. "This one you have got to hear," continued her dad. "I'll tell you the whole story, but first I think we better show mommy your gift and give her one too, and a big hug and a kiss, so she won't feel left out. Oh, and I need to pay the babysitter. 'Amanda!'" yelled Mr. Evans.

"Amanda's upstairs getting her stuff," Reilly quickly informed. "And Mommy will be home from work in a little bit. She's bringing our favorite Chinese food. Then you can tell Mommy and me the story! You better go wash your hands and get ready for supper!"

"Right, you are the boss!" Mr. Evans responded. "You better do likewise. I think I hear Mommy pulling up right now!" He then tickled her stomach, and they both laughed.

Later that night, Reilly, her mother, and dad sat at the dinner table with boxes of Chinese food scattered around. Reilly was busy playing with the toy dragon and knight.

Mr. Evans picked up the toy dragon and began the story. "Let me tell you about this special dragon now… the old man in the shop started by saying that this little dragon was indeed the bravest dragon there has ever been in all the history of the world! You see honey, the old man said that back when dragons lived on earth, there were mainly two kinds… dragons that ate plants… and dragons that ate meat. The meat-eating dragons used to terrorize the people that lived back then. They could use their fire breath to burn down a whole village."

Reilly looked worried, but her father smiled and continued, "Don't worry honey… there was a wizard named Merlinius who protected the people. There were also these royal knights whose main job was to hunt down bad dragons, capture them and take them away. Then one day, a war between the two different kinds of dragons broke out! The war just about brought an end to the existence of all of the dragons on earth forever and ever! That's where the wizard and your little dragon come in…"

"What is a wizard, Daddy?" Reilly asked.

Her father laughed and replied, "A wizard is a person who has magical powers!"

"Like a magician?" asked Reilly.

"Yes, like that, but even more powerful," Mr. Evans replied. "Powerful enough to tame a dragon or make a whole town disappear, or topple towers and create storms!"

"Wow!" Reilly exclaimed.

"Wow indeed!" continued Mr. Evans. "Now, let's tell this story all the way to the end before Mommy tucks you in."

Mr. Evans picked the child up and gently took her over to kiss his wife as she put the leftovers away. Then the two of them went over to an easy chair near the fireplace. The father sat down first, then had Reilly climb up on his lap. Suddenly, there was a loud clap of thunder and lightning flashes outside the window.

"Listen to that!!" Mr. Evans exclaimed. "You know that when there is a storm and a blinding flash of light shoots across the sky…

everyone calls that lightning? Well, guess what that blinding light really is?"

"What?" asked Reilly.

"It's fire coming out of a dragon's mouth!" Mr. Evans exclaimed.

Reilly was amazed. "Can dragons really breathe fire?" "Yes," he replied, nodding his head up and down.

Mr. Evans then asked, "Guess what else? You know that loud noise we call thunder?"

Reilly slowly nodded her head 'yes.'

Mr. Evans continued, "That's a dragon roaring with all its might!" "Why are dragons breathing fire and roaring so loud, Daddy? Are they fighting?"

"Yes, as a matter of fact, that's right, they are fighting!" Reilly's father explained. "They also sometimes cause tornadoes when they're fighting!"

"How Daddy?" Reilly asked, looking puzzled.

"Well, when two dragons are fighting to get their tails untangled, their wings flap wildly and cause them to spin around and around out of control… and then… voila! You have a tornado!"

Reilly queried her father, "You're telling me a fib, aren't you Daddy?"

"Oh no, baby," he responded convincingly. "Let me tell you more of what the old man told me about a time long ago. A time when dragons were still alive on earth, and the people decided to get rid of them.…"

CHAPTER 2

On a great island in the midst of the Terra Median Sea, lies the Kindgom of Albion. It's a rainy afternoon by the grove side in the Albion meadow, the funeral of Sir Jonathan is taking place, by orders of the King, all Royal Knight Funerals are Held in Secrecy. Fewer than twenty people were attendance. One of those attending was the King of Albion, King Arturus.

Also attending was Sir Jonathan's widow, whose name was Jaysha, and Sir Jonathan's only child, a young boy named David. The rest of those in attendance were other royal knights, including a royal knight who was with Sir Jonathan when he was slain. His name was Sir Solomon, and he had now taken Sir Jonathon's place as the king's first Royal Knight at Arms.

As the priest finished the ceremony, he rolls up his scroll, and the crowd begins to disperse. As King Arturus passed by Sir Jonathan's widow, he suddenly stopped.

"He will forever be remembered in stone," said the king emphatically, staring into the sad eyes of Jaysha.

"HE—had a name… Jonathan!!" Jaysha screamed in contempt. Silently, the king walked away, and Sir Solomon rebuffed Jaysha,

"What's wrong with you? No one talks to the king like that!"

"What king?" Jaysha scornfully replied. "A king wouldn't send his best knight to certain death!"

Sir Solomon worried, "Speaking those words could put you in line for certain death, Jaysha! You know the royal knights don't ever truly die. We are all sworn to uphold the king's orders. What happened to Jon wasn't the fault of King Arturus, nor was it Jon's, nor was it mine. It was the fault of those vicious dragons!"

That evening, in the Albion forest, Jaysha's young boy, David, walked through the bushes yelling, "Rago! Rago!!"

From within a thicket of trees, a dragon followed closely through the underbrush, watching David. Just as David passed the predator, the gigantic monster jumped mid-air and pounced on David, knocking him down. David started to laugh at the dragon, which was no bigger than a dog. Rago was David's pet dragon.

"Stop it, Rago!" laughed David as Rago licked his face. "Ok, ok, I'm happy to see you too!" David got to his feet, dusting off the leaves and dirt. Rago danced around, much like a happy dog would. David and Rago were soon walking about exploring the countryside. Coming upon some large rocks, they both stopped, and David sat down.

David said, "Rago, I have something to tell you. It's now too dangerous for you to remain here." Rago gave David a confused look as David continued. "You see, the king has given an order to kill all dragons on sight! A meat-eater killed my father." Rago stomped his feet and swung his head. David continued, "I know, I know, Rago, your kind doesn't kill humans. But the people don't understand that! To them, all dragons are evil killers."

Rago appeared very distressed as David continued, "It's not safe for you to come here anymore. You and your family have to leave here and go as far away as you can." David and Rago embraced, for they loved one another dearly.

David reassured, "I have to get back before my mother comes looking for me." Rago stomped his feet and swung back and forth. David continued, "It will be okay. We will see each other again my friend. Don't worry."

David turned and started to jog toward a house at the other end of the meadow. Rago, whimpering much like a dog would, turned and walked away, disappearing behind trees and bushes.

CHAPTER 3

David came running into the front yard of Jaysha's house around noon. At the same time, Sir Solomon galloped toward the house on his horse.

David reached the house first and turned to watch Sir Solomon dismount from his horse and approach him.

"Hello David, how are you? How are you holding up?" Sir Solomon asked in a very compassionate tone.

"Good, but I miss my dad…" replied David.

"He misses you too."

"He can't be missing me," protested David. "My mom told me the truth. He died, no matter what the king says."

"Speaking of your mother, I need to talk to her," said Sir Solomon. "Is she here?"

"I think so, she was when I left. Hold on, I'll go see."

David turned and ran inside, leaving the front door open. Sir Solomon slowly walked to the front door to wait. A moment later, he saw Jaysha walking toward the door.

"What are you doing here?" Jaysha asked.

"I have something that needs to be said," Sir Solomon replied with conviction. "Jon would insist that I talk to you."

"Oh please, how would you know what Jon would insist on? Jaysha dismissed the idea with a wave of her hand and a look of disgust. "And that is Sir Jonathan to you."

"Jaysha, I don't deserve to be treated like this!" Sir Solomon responded, perplexed at Jaysha's behavior toward him. "Jon and I were best friends. That monster was lying in wait, and the trees made numerous shadows; there was no way we could have seen that vicious beast."

There was a moment of silence as Jaysha absorbed the information. Jaysha then asked, "Is that it, are you done?"

"Have I ever, ever been disrespectful to you; have I ever been disrespectful in *any way*?" asked Sir Solomon.

"No, you haven't," responded Jaysha, with resignation in her voice. Jaysha turned and walked toward the center of the room. She then looked back over her shoulder and asked Sir Solomon to come in. Sir Solomon shook the dirt from his heels and walked inside.

Jaysha sat down and motioned for Sir Solomon to take his place across from her.

"I realize I haven't been fair to you," Jaysha started. "It's just that I am so angry, so frustrated. How could King Arturus send his best man to kill dragons? It is certain death. Why was Jon out at night? What was so important that he had to be hunting at night?"

"Jon wanted to come home," Sir Solomon replied. "We had been hunting this certain vicious dragon for weeks. Jon thought he knew where the dragon would be and it would most likely be sleeping if we could find the beast at night. You know Jon wanted nothing more than to come home to you and David."

"What I came to say is that…" Solomon paused, and then stood up. "When Jon and I first became royal knights, we made a vow, an oath, that if either of us were to die, the other would provide for and take care of his surviving family. I wanted to let you know that I am going to honor that oath, just as Jon surely would have done the same for me."

"That is very honorable of you, considering you don't have a family," Jaysha replied, her tone now much softer. "I admire the fact that you want to keep the vow you made to Jonathan. However, I must kindly decline your offer, as I won't be needing it. You see, my husband's absence has made me, out of necessity, become quite independent."

"I am certainly aware that you are capable," Sir Solomon replied. "But I wouldn't be Jon's friend if I didn't come and offer any help you may need."

"In Respect of my dead husband, I thank you for your offer." There was silence while Jaysha digested this olive branch offered by her dead husband's best friend. Solomon began to feel he was in danger of overstaying his welcome and slowly rose and turned toward the door. Just as Solomon was about to step out, he heard soft whimpering. He turned to see Jaysha starting to cry. He quickly ran to her and Jaysha embraced Solomon, hanging on him while sobbing uncontrollably. "I miss him, Solomon, I miss him so much."

"I do too, Jaysha, I do too."

Jaysha cried in Solomon 's arms for a while before Sir Solomon finally disentangled himself and said goodbye.

The following day, in a beautiful vast meadow surrounded by pine trees, and covered by a two-foot thick layer of dense fog, a low rumble was heard. Ordinarily, the meadow was so quiet that all that could be heard were a few birds chirping and a woodpecker pecking in the background.

But on this day the rumbling sound began to grow louder and louder. A posse of five royal knights could be seen galloping on a path that cut through a dense growth of pine trees. They, along with the horses they were riding, were dressed in full body armor. The horses' hooves pounded the ground as they galloped down the path.

The rumbling sound grew louder and louder, eventually turning into a thunder. The posse of royal knights came galloping out from within the thick growth of pine trees.

The horses' hooves kept rising up out of the thick layer of fog and then quickly back down. The armor clamored from the royal knights and horses, as pieces of dirt flew from the hooves that pounded into the ground.

The posse of royal knights crossed the meadow and then disappeared back into the forest on the opposite side.

The posse of royal knights rode up to a huge canyon which cut through the forest landscape. The canyon had a prehistoric look to it, with very jagged edges and steep cliffs. The group came to an abrupt stop at the edge of a cliff.

The leader of the posse was Sir Solomon. He observed a river flowing at the bottom of the vast canyon below. His eyes followed the river until he saw an opening of a large cave at the bottom of the canyon.

Sir Solomon gestured with his arm for his knights to spread out and then waved for them to descend down into the canyon. A couple of knights still mounted on their horses trotted off to the side while Sir Solomon and two other knights rode down a narrow path. At one side of the trail, there was a hundred foot vertical drop to the bottom of the canyon.

Sir Solomon and the two knights reached the bottom of the canyon and started dismounting, quickly taking their swords out of their sheaths. A couple of them pulled out unlit torches.

They slowly entered the cave and, one by one, disappeared into the darkness of the cave's interior.

Sir Solomon bent down and struck flint together, causing sparks to fly. After a few strikes, he was able to get a small fire going. He then grabbed one of the unlit torches and caught it on fire.

With torches burning bright, the three knights walked deeper into the cave. The walls of the cave widened as the knights continued marching deeper within.

One of the knights produced a bag from a pouch and ignited it. He threw the lit bag far out into the darkness and, when it hit the ground, it burst silently into a giant bonfire. The light exposed a cavernous room. With great astonishment, the knights beheld five huge dragons sleeping near each other at one end of the vast chamber. By this time the three knights had been joined by the two others, who were at the opposite side of the large cavern. The two signaled to Sir Solomon, who in turn signaled back to them to continue their advance forward.

With the bonfire burning bright, all five knights quietly approached the sleeping dragons. As they moved closer, they took note of the particular species of dragon they had discovered.

This species had horns that stuck out from the sides of their heads and continued down their necks. They also had horns on their shoulders and backs. Their wings were like those of bats, bony and leathery. The sound of the dragons' snoring was like thunder.

One of the dragons' eyes suddenly popped open. The startled dragon started to lift its head, but his head was stopped by a sword's tip piercing the top of it.

Simultaneously, each knight sank their swords into each dragon's head, killing them instantly. One of the dragons was no more than a baby.

In the middle of a large lake, several boats sat with numerous knights aboard. The knights were standing ready as if waiting for something to happen at any moment.

Suddenly, a few bubbles began to rise to the surface of the water, soon followed by a rush of huge bubbles.

A considerable object burst out from the depths of the lake.

The water dragon, which in legend is known as a sea serpent, has gills for ears and teeth like a piranha's. A large fin extends from its shoulder and narrows down to its webbed claws. The water dragon now towered over one of the boats.

The well-trained knights immediately began throwing spears; many of which hit their targeted area on the dragon's upper torso. The water dragon began to sway back and forth and then plunged its head, crashing it directly into the middle of one of the boats. The dragon then lifted its head up again, holding a knight in the razor-sharp teeth of its mouth.

The near-demolished boat was still adrift, with some of the knights grabbing hold of parts of it. One of them, foolishly dressed in full armor, yelled as he lost his hold on a large piece of the wrecked boat. The weight of his armor caused the knight to sink immediately.

Another knight leaped and threw himself onto the dragon's head, beginning to repeatedly stab the water dragon in the eye.

The water dragon roared in anguish as the other knights continuously slashed and stabbed at its body with their swords. The dragon eventually collapsed back into the water. Moments later, it came floating up to the surface, dead.

Later that evening, a few knights gathered around a conference table in the middle of a large room. The knights suspended their conversation as footsteps were heard coming toward them.

Wearing his royal robe and crown, King Arturus, the king of Albion, a great island in the midst of the Terra Median Sea, entered the room, followed by two royal knights wearing armor so polished the other knights could see their image in it.

The door had been opened by a knight posted at the doorway. The royal knights rose to stand at attention as the king walked over to them. They pounded their chests with their right hand and exchanged greetings with their king.

"All hail King Arturus of Albion!" the knights greeted enthusiastically.

King Arturus responded, "I received word that you're carrying out my orders magnificently!"

"Yes, Your Majesty," replied Sir Solomon. "The men are on a quest to wipe out all the dragons in the kingdom, as you required of them. If they fought like this against all of our human enemies, you would be the ruler of the world, Your Majesty!"

Sir Solomon then took out and unfolded a large map which he proceeded to lay on the table. Everyone in the room gathered around the map that was spread out on the conference table.

Sir Solomon began to point to spots on the map of Albion. "Here, here and here, Your Majesty, the vicious dragons are all dead. All dragons have been almost totally annihilated by sword and spear from these territories in Albion east of the great city of Falconhold. In the West, arrows dipped in poison loosed by your noble woodsmen have been very successful in killing off the woodland dragons, Your Majesty."

"Good!" shouted King Arturus, smiling with delight. "You're doing magnificent work, Sir Solomon. I see your quest coming to a quick and successful end! We will have a great feast in honor of the order of the royal knights of Albion. Gold will be given to all of your men as well for their exemplary service to their king!"

"Thank you, Your Majesty," Sir Solomon said as he bowed deeply. "The men will be eternally grateful. A wondrous feast will do all the people of Albion a great deal of good! Sadly, many people lost many loved ones during the dragons' evil tyranny."

"I do know their pain," replied King Arturus. "A great feast it shall be then, a feast of thanksgiving… for the entire kingdom! There shall be much mead, dancing maidens, jugglers, fools and jousts in their honor. Let it be done as I command in one fortnight!"

"As you command, my liege," responded Sir Solomon, gathering up the map and gesturing to the other knights that it was time to leave. They quickly made haste to obey the unspoken order, filing out in ranks and shutting the great door behind them.

In the Albion wilderness, a group of dragons was drinking from a stream and eating plant growth which covered the surrounding area. Several knights dipped arrows into a wooden bucket filled with a red colored liquid and surrounded the dragons as they had been given orders to do. A knight, under cover of the bushes, saw an unsuspecting dragon lying down. The knights prepared to attack, each one of them signaling to the other.

"Attack!!" screamed one of the knights.

The knights charged toward the unsuspecting dragon, shooting the tainted arrows. Arrows penetrated the dragon's tough reptilian skin, and pierced its flesh.

The largest dragon charged the knights like an elephant protecting its herd. But the enormous dragon began to slow to a halt, then collapsed to the ground, lying helpless.

A knight rushed to the powerless beast and raised his sword, making a swift but forceful stab into the dragon's head.

The other dragons, rendered helpless from the poisoned arrows, all collapsed to the ground and were quickly killed by the knights.

Later, in a meeting room, several people were gathered around a map showing the whole island continent of Albion. The map was spread out on top of a table, and half of it appeared to be blacked out.

Present at this meeting, wearing a very colorful robe, was an older man with long white hair and a long white beard. His name was Merlinius, and he was the most powerful wizard of all time. Merlinius furiously stomped away from the people gathered around the map, for he was decidedly against the killing of the dragons.

King Arturus stood in the background next to the table, along with two royal knights. The door to the conference room swung open, allowing Sir Solomon to march in, followed by a group of knights. It appeared that the knights and Merlinius would walk straight into each other, but at the last minute, Sir Solomon, followed by the knights, stepped clearly to the side, giving Merlinius plenty of room to pass. Unfortunately, one disrespectful knight seemed bent on intentionally walking straight into Merlinius. Merlinius did not budge. Instead, he shoved the knight effortlessly, sending him flying to the ground. The knight got up in anger and drew his sword. With Merlinius' back towards him, the knight lifted his sword up and ran toward Merlinius, intending to kill the old man.

Merlinius turned swiftly with his eyes watching the attacking knight. He raised his staff and pointed it at his attacker. The knight suddenly stopped his charge toward Merlinius, freezing in his tracks. His armor began to shrink. His face showed anguish as his armor continuously shrank. The unfortunate knight's bones were overheard breaking as he was slowly squeezed to death. Blood oozed from within the crushed armor of the knight, following the cracks of the stone floor. Then the knight's armor simply vaporized, as did his body and blood. One of the knights approached the king with pleading eyes, "Your Majesty, you can't just let Merlinius kill one of our best men!"

"How can I stop a power that I cannot see?!" retorted King Arturus. "Merlinius is the greatest wizard ever known! He could be king of Albion if he wanted to. Only an utter fool would seek his life in open combat like that! Sir Manfred got his just desserts."

Merlinius then left the king's castle. And walks down a path in a wooded area, As he was walking, Merlinius suddenly vanished, leaving only a puff of sparkles. Amazingly, Sir Manfred appeared where Merlinius had just been standing! He thrust his sword at nothing, then stood amazed and utterly puzzled.

Weeks later the knights returned to the conference room. The total annihilation of the dragons was near completion. The map of Albion that was half blacked out was now entirely blacked out. Word had continually come in that dragons had vanished from everywhere in the kingdom. King Arturus and a few knights were laughing and drinking, boasting of the successful massacre of all the dragons on the continent.

Sir Solomon enthused, "I hope that self-righteous Merlinius finally realizes that he isn't always right!"

"Yes, indeed, even Merlinius himself couldn't go against an entire kingdom," replied the king.

"To all the people of Albion!" the king shouted, raising his goblet of wine.

Turning aside to whisper to Solomon, he continued, "Imagine, wanting to let the dragons live." King Arturus sighed and said, "Sir Manfred died terribly, being squeezed to death by the very armor that was designed to save him! What Irony! Haha! Irony!? Don't you see? Because armor is iron… oh never mind. Poor man, he knew Merlinius was outraged over the mass killings of his precious dragons… and yet he foolishly challenged him!"

"I agree my king!" Sir Solomon replied. "But, if it pleases your grace, Sir Manfred was found not a mile from your castle yesterday wandering around, completely mad! He keeps saying he is a ghost! So apparently Merlinius did not slay him at all but rather put on a show for our entertainment… yet I fear that as a knight he is now completely useless to us. He cannot stand the sight of swords or armor. He runs away, and he lives as a hermit in the woods."

"That is a lesson to us all," King Arturus responded. "We must be wary of a mage who can make us see things that do not exist and who can turn a well- trained soldier into a blithering madman! For now, however, let us revel in our victory over the vicious dragons of Albion!"

"Yes, my lord," answered Sir Solomon. "Enough of what has been. Let's enjoy and celebrate our success as you had foretold. Huzzah! King Arturus!"

"Huzzah, King Arturus!" everyone shouted as they raised their goblets.

CHAPTER 4

Merlinius stood in a room where books lined all four walls and where candles burned on every table and shelf. At one side of the room stood three tables with large crystal balls set up on each of them. A different dimension appeared inside each one of the crystal balls.

One of the crystal balls showed what was currently happening in Albion, which included the dragons being killed throughout the land. Another crystal ball showed electrons shooting around. A third crystal ball showed a spaceship landing on a barren planet with strange aliens coming out of the spaceship. Yet another crystal ball showed mutant-like creatures moving about through barren land.

Merlinius' face reflected different colors from the different pictures that were manifesting through the crystal balls. He witnessed five baby dragons being mercilessly slaughtered by royal knights in one crystal ball. Merlinius muttered under his breath, "In all these dimensions of time, the present displays the most cruelty."

Overwhelmed with anger, Merlinius picked up a porcelain vase and threw it against the wall, smashing it to pieces. After a few moments, the wizard gathered himself and walked out onto the balcony of the study.

Merlinius stared out toward tiny lights scattered throughout the landscape, which were actually lit torches in front of the stone dwellings where people lived. The incandescent lamps were spread throughout the entire kingdom of Albion.

Merlinius thought to himself, "I know the evil ways of some dragons are inexcusable, but that's not enough reason to kill an entire species. But how can I get through to these people that some dragons are harmless, even friendly? All they see are dragons eating their livestock, and yes, they have eaten people from time to time. But dragons are not evil demons, they're only a large species of the reptile."

He shook his head, "These people just have no idea. Still, it's no use going against the will of an entire kingdom! Almost all the dragons are gone now, anyway."

The following morning a posse of royal knights galloped their horses through the forest. Coming upon a narrow canyon, the knights descended down to a bridge, and crossed in single file.

When the last knight finished crossing the bridge, the branches underneath the bridge at the bottom of the canyon could be seen shaking with aggressive movement.

The knights galloped away, continuing their way through the forest. A family of five plant-eating dragons emerged from behind huge boulders and from under large trees at the bottom of the canyon. The five dragons were obviously hiding from the knights that were crossing the bridge. The most massive dragon, whose name was Dagger, began to speak to the other dragons. To Humans, The Dragon Speaking Simply Sounds Like Growling "Whew!" he exclaimed, looking up towards the bridge. "That was close!

Come on, enough time has been wasted already!"

The family of dragons started up the rocky path, cautiously proceeding so as not to allow themselves to be seen.

One of the dragons was younger and much smaller than the others. He was Rago, David's friend. As Rago began to tire from the long journey, a giant dragon came over and nudged him. This massive dragon was Deetha, Rago's mother. She urged her young dragon to keep going, which Rago reluctantly did.

In the evening the family of dragons finally came to a halt. Looking up, they saw a gigantic stone castle on the plateau of a high mountain peak. The mountainside had very steep cliffs and jagged slopes, which provided natural protection for those residing in the castle.

Dagger looked toward the family of dragons. "We'll take cover here and wait until nightfall," stated Dagger.

The family of dragons looked around and then split apart, finding cover under the trees, in small caves, or behind huge rocks. The day had ended, the shelter of the night had finally arrived.

The next morning, at the bottom of the mountain, the family of dragons came together for a few moments. They dared not risk using their wings to fly up to the castle for fear of being seen by any royal knights who may be scouting the area. There was also the possibility of other dragons or villagers being in the area. There was simply no place to hide in the skies. So, in single file, they all started up a dangerous trail which led to the castle on top of the mountain. Again, Rago stalled, but his mother nudged her baby forward. Reluctantly, Rago continued up the mountain trail.

By afternoon the family of dragons was near their destination. The trail had turned into nothing more than a narrow ledge which cut through the side of the vertical cliff. Fear could be seen on Rago's face, his eyes were glued downward where the jagged vertical cliff disappeared into a blanket of low lying clouds. His legs twitched, as he fought the impulse to turn around and run for his dear life. His heart sank, knowing that he had yet to learn the art of flying like older dragons.

Rago looked downward and thought, *It would be certain death if I slipped and fell. I wish I had paid attention to those flying lessons, mom tried to teach me.* Rago shuddered, looking at his small wings.

Returning to the journey at hand, part of the trail gave way underneath him, sending Rago instantly straight down. In a panic,

Rago began flapping his wings as hard as he could, trying to fly. With his heart pumping, his head spinning, and lungs bursting, his body screamed for survival. Every muscle craved relaxation as blood coursed through his veins and his pulse quickened. Rago had no other choice and, much to his surprise, his downward fall began to dramatically slow down and then completely stop. Rago, for the first time, was flying on his own. He started flying upward and was greeted by his mother, Deetha, who had flown down to rescue her baby. They both returned to the other dragons where they were greeted by Dagger, who was Rago's father.

"You must be more careful, son," said Dagger to Rago, with concern in his voice. "For we can't be seen. But at last, you can fly!"

"Yeah, who knew?" replied Rago, as the family of dragons continued walking on the narrow trail up the mountain.

CHAPTER 5

The family of dragons finally reached the magnificent castle of Merlinius. The entrance gate began to slowly open, and the dragons gingerly entered the castle, one by one. They then entered into a huge room, which was Merlinius' alchemical laboratory.

The room was filled with numerous tables which had hundreds of glass alchemy retorts, tubes, flasks, and other necessary items arranged on them. Merlinius gestured with his hands to Dagger, who then shook his head and hit his front foot onto the ground.

They began to have a conversation though only Merlinius was speaking out loud. Merlinius was able to hear Dagger's thoughts using telepathy, a typical power possessed by all wizards.

"If I do this, Dagger, you and your family will all have to stay in the clouds for the rest of your lives!" Merlinius said forcefully. "You must never come down during the daytime."

"We'll manage, but how can we find enough food in the darkness?" Dagger asked.

"You'll have to take advantage of full moons and eat up… it's the best I can do," Merlinius replied.

"Hmm…" Dagger paused. "Let me talk with my family in private."

Dagger went over to his family, and they huddled around him. A rumbling noise began from within the huddle of dragons as they expressed their anger at the prospect of not having the use of daylight to find edible plants to eat. Despite their noisy complaints, Dagger returned quickly to finish the deal with Merlinius.

"I suppose we have no other choice but to come down only at night to feed and feel the earth," Dagger told Merlinius. "We will do as you've said. Though I wish there were another way…"

The matter being settled, Merlinius patted Dagger on the chest.

But Merlinius and the dragons were not alone. A younger man, named Odious, had been hiding in the laboratory closet, spying on Merlinius and the dragon family through a cracked door.

Odious was in an apprenticeship for wizardry under Merlinius but was always up to no good. He had a secret hidden agenda, desiring to become the most powerful wizard in all of history.

From his secret hiding place, Odious was amazed to see Merlinius gather jars of luminescent powder and then begin to perform a magical spell with his focus on the dragon family.

Merlinius waved his magic wand in circles. He then grabbed the different colored luminescent powders from the jars he had gathered and tossed the radiant powder all over the family of dragons. Speckled, colored lights began to swirl around the dragons. Merlinius chanted mystical words as he performed the magic spell.

"I command the stars above and the wind below to combine with the wings of an eagle and the soul of a dragon henceforth and defy the power of the sun and its planets. Let the power possessed by gravity have no more effect on any dragon within the boundaries of this room!"

"What in the world is going on?" Odious whispered to himself, unable to contain his astonishment as he watched Merlinius cast the spell on the dragons.

Each dragon began to levitate up off the laboratory floor. Merlinius' face dripped with sweat created during his performance. Merlinius smiled as he watched the family of dragons floating entirely off the ground, all suspended in the air.

Odious opened the door of the closet a little more in order to get a better view of this astonishing sight. He had never seen nor heard of any spell that could make living things weightless.

The family of dragons appeared to be very elated, some of them nudging each other with their noses. One of them rolled over upside down playfully, but soon began to yelp, and quickly turned back over. He swayed back and forth, having been made dizzy by the playful exercise of his new ability. Dagger, the father, laughed at the smaller dizzy dragon.

Merlinius walked over and released a chain which allowed a section of the laboratory wall to slide open, exposing the outside world. Outside of the laboratory was a breathtaking view of a magnificent mountain range, with the highest of its cloud-covered peaks glistening in the light of a full moon. The dragons floated over to Merlinius, who was standing at the edge of the opened wall admiring the majestic view. Merlinius pointed toward the skies, "There's your family's new home Dagger…" He turned to Dagger, smiling, "You and your family will find refuge there. Go now, before anyone comes and sees what I have done!"

Dagger nodded in agreement to Merlinius, then bowed in respect. Dagger then looked toward the other dragons and gestured for them to go. One by one, each dragon nodded to Merlinius as they floated away through the opening in the wall.

Rago went over to Merlinius and licked him on the cheek. Merlinius, in turn, gave Rago a hug and then sent him on his way.

The dragons floated up, up and away. As they flew away, Merlinius whispered to himself, "Remember our agreement, my friend. For you and your family can never be seen again by men."

Suddenly, Dagger sensed Merlinius' concern and looked back down towards the castle. With gratitude in his voice, he said, "Don't worry my friend. We will keep well hidden in our new home, the clouds!"

Merlinius' face showed his concern for his dear friends. He watched the dragons grow smaller and smaller as they ascended to the sky and disappeared into the high clouds. "I did the right thing… I had no choice!" Merlinius told himself.

The family of dragons was now able to float and soar higher than ever through the skies with the greatest of ease. They flew into clouds which were beautifully silhouetted by a very bright full moon which lit up the entire horizon. The entire family disappeared into the dense fog cover of the clouds.

That night Merlinius retired for bed earlier than usual, exhausted by his performance. Shortly after lying down, he suddenly sprang up in his bed, being alerted by something in the room. He carefully listened as he looked all about his dark room.

Merlinius' laboratory that night was dark and empty. Only the jars of luminescent powder lit the room where he had conducted the magic spell. The silhouette of a man could be seen approaching the glowing jars of bright powder.

The man was Odious. His face was lit up by the reflecting changing colors of light coming from the jars. He took a closer look at the ingredients used during the magic spell of weightlessness. Odious said to himself, "I wonder if…"

Odious hurriedly gathered the jars and put them into a sack, immediately causing the sack to glow from the light of the luminescent powder. Odious dashed out of the laboratory with the bag in hand.

Within moments, Odious fled the castle out a back door. He headed off down a path and disappeared around a ridge.

Descending down a narrow path on the mountainside, Odious finally reached a cave. He stopped at the entrance to light a torch before cautiously going inside.

The narrow walls of the cave, made visible by the lit torch, gradually began to widen as Odious walked along. He eventually reached a large room deep within the cavern. From the light of the burning torch, he could see several dragons lying down asleep. They were hiding deep within the cave, seeking to escape the massacring of their species in the outside world. Their razor-sharp teeth clearly evidenced that they were meat eaters.

This group of dragons had two primary leaders, one named Zindetha, and the other Deman. Zindetha awakened first, and a telepathic communication ensued between Odious and the dragons.

"Zindetha, I have something I believe you'll like!" exclaimed Odious.

"Odious, what is it? A goat?! I'm hungry!" bellowed Zindetha.

"No! This is better than a goat."

"Oh?" Zindetha replied, unimpressed. "A royal knight is tasty!"

"Afraid not, you gross monster! You'll have to get that on your own."

Deman looked up and saw that it was just the same stupid human that sometimes brought them food.

"Quit playing games, human! Just leave whatever it is and…"

Odious interrupted Deman, "I have a way to make all of you weightless!"

"Weightless? You mean like float?" inquired Deman, with keen interest.

"Yes, exactly! You'll be able to escape the killing going on by being able to hide in the clouds."

Deman went over to Odious, lowering his head and looking him squarely in the eyes. "You better not try anything foolish!"

"How dare you talk to me like that, you beast? I almost possess the full powers of a wizard. And when I do, I will be your master!"

Zindetha roared loudly to interrupt them. Deman looked back to see what his companion wanted. Zindetha gave Deman the evil eye, reminding him that they needed to be kind to their human friend, at least for now. "Forgive me… master."

Deman turned away, almost barfing from disgust. He walked over to Zindetha with an appalled look on his face. Deman and Zindetha talked for a few moments, then Zindetha returned to Odious.

"We're ready to try this weightlessness, or whatever it is that will make us able to live up in the clouds… as you have said."

"First, I want two things understood. First, if I do this, you must only come down to eat at night. Also, I want full obedience and command of all of you! I will indeed be the master of dragons. Or… or I can easily reverse the spell and let the royal knights of Albion hunt you down."

"Odious, grant us this magic power of yours, and you will have your command!"

Odious excitedly asked Zindetha to gather the dragons together. Zindetha walked over and talked to Deman, who nodded his head. The two leaders went and gathered all the other dragons. They all then slowly went over to Odious who was smiling, not because of feelings of happiness, but because of the feeling of power. Odious spread out the jars of the different luminescent powders and then pulled out Merlinius' magic wand and started to chant.

"I command the stars above and wind below to with… with… uh…" Odious seemed to forget part of the spell. "…Wings of an eagle and the soul of a dragon to… to defy the power of the sun and its planets. Let the power possessed by gravity be no more for any dragon within…. within the boundaries of this roo-er, cave!"

All of a sudden, the dragons started to levitate. Odious, the apprentice had been successful. The dragons looked under themselves and then at each other. The dragons all began to make rumbling sounds like that of rolling thunder. Odious, astonished with himself that the spell had worked, picked up the lit torch. Suddenly, the light given off from the flame was drowned out by a series of blinding bright flashes. The dragons were forcing Odious to leave the cave by striking their breath- fires at his feet. Odious began to back up, but decided to give his command, "Stay in the cave until I return!"

Deman defiantly told Odious to get out of his way. Zindetha told Odious that he was foolish to have given them the power of levitation, leaving Odious with nothing.

"I demand you to obey my command! Or I will reverse the magic spell and tell the king where you are hiding!" Odious screamed, panic-stricken. He began waving the wand as if to cast a spell, but the dragons all continued to defy him.

The dragons started to float towards Odious, backing him against the cavern wall. Deman made a swoop towards Odious and tried to take a bite out of him.

"Hehehe! Goodbye to you, almost a wizard! You can tell your grandchildren if you live that long, that you were once almost eaten by a dragon!"

Odious dove behind a stalagmite for cover. Deman landed quickly and continued to try to bite Odious, his razor-sharp teeth repeatedly snapping, barely missing Odious' flesh. Feeling helpless and unable to stop the dragons, Odious realized that he had no idea how to reverse the spell. Suddenly, Zindetha gave her command to the dragons.

"Deman, forget about the human, let's get up to the clouds where we have cover. Merlinius will come after his foolish student soon enough, and sooner or later he'll come after us."

All the dragons floated past the terrified Odious on their way out. When the dragons were gone, Odious ran out of the cave. He stopped to watch the dragons.

Flying upward toward the mountain range in the far distance, the dragons ascended until they reached the clouds high above, coming in and out of view as they entered the heavy fog cover of the clouds until the last one disappeared into the heavens.

Odious realized that he had made an awful decision in granting the meat- eating dragons the magic of weightlessness. He ran back inside the cave, then returned moments later, carrying the bag of glowing jars of luminescent powder. Odious quickly traversed the trail back up to Merlinius' castle. He stopped at the castle's entrance and then slowly opened the door.

Looking inside Merlinius' castle before going in, Odious surveyed the dark silence, checking to make sure the coast was clear. *Yes!* he thought to himself, *The old crow is probably in his nest sleeping.* He entered the castle.

The laboratory was dark except for a moving, glowing sack which was now set upon a table. Odious opened his bag and started to put the luminescent jars away when he was startled by Merlinius suddenly walking in. Merlinius was suspicious of his apprentice, but could not put a finger on what exactly was the matter.

"Odious, what are you doing in here?"

"Sir, your bottles of this glowing powder are interesting to me. I guess curiosity got the best of me."

Merlinius walked over to him, suspecting that Odious was up to something, but not able to figure out quite what it was this time. "Where have you been? I was looking for you earlier."

"I forgot I had to meet a friend in town! And when I remembered, I didn't have enough time to find you… so I just left. Sir, what is in these jars?"

"Gases, chemicals, and other things."

"Really?" asked Odious, picking up a jar and pretending to examine it with keen interest.

"Well, my friend is meeting me at the tavern in the morning. I think I'll call it a night... oh... so tired." Faking a yawn, and stretching, he continued, "You didn't want those jars arranged in any certain color or way, did you? No, I didn't think so! Well off to my loft! Heh, long night..."

Odious quickly walked away, trying to leave before Merlinius could ask any more questions. Merlinius watched him walk farther away before blurting out, "How are your studies coming?"

"Good, I'm almost done with the whole magical broom trick! Heh. What jolly good fun that is, having a broom that sweeps up all by itself... or a mop, mopping... I'm tired master. ... Long day tomorrow! Nighty night!"

Odious turned away, muttering under his breath, "I should have told the old crow that I performed the spell of weightlessness as good as he did!"

Chapter 6

The crusade of the extinction of dragons was over, and the celebration which the king had promised was in full swing in the city of Falconhold in Albion.

"A toast!" yelled a knight, while raising his goblet. "To the end of all the dragons! And long live the king!"

"Long live the king!!" swelled the chorus of numerous knights in response, with raised goblets in the air. Loud talking and laughter could be overheard throughout the festival.

From the cloudy sky above Albion, Rago's head popped out from within a cloud, being filled with curiosity at all the celebratory noise. Startled by what he saw, Rago quickly pulled his head back inside the cloud. Dagger was breathing down Rago's neck within the dense mist of the clouds.

"I cannot have you disobeying me, son! You must never go beyond the cover of the clouds during the daytime."

"I'm sorry, papa," Rago replied with his head down. I promise to never do that again… I'm just so hungry."

"Now don't get started, Rago. You know we have to wait till nightfall… now let's get back before your mother gets worried."

They both drifted off into the heavy mist and faded away.

Zindetha and Deman were joined by a third meat eater, named Sadan.

All three dragons began a discussion from the opposite side of the clouds where Rago and his father had just left.

Zindetha looked puzzledly at Deman and Sadan, "Where did they come from? They must have gotten help from Merlinius. That stupid human Odious must have gotten the magic spell he used on us from him!"

"If those plant eaters ever see us, we will have to kill them before they can tell Merlinius!" Deman suggested.

"It sounds good to me! Young dragon meat is juicy!" Sadan replied excitedly. Sadan roared with excitement so loud that It sounded like thunder. Apparently, the magic spell amplified the dragon's vocal cords.

Down below the celebration was in full swing. The dragon's roar was heard by only a few, because of all the loud cheering going on. Those who heard looked up and then around to see what made the loud boom, one person questioning another, "Did you hear that?"

"Hear what?" the other asked.

Both shrugged and then continued with their partying.

In the countryside of Albion, nearly everyone heard the sound from Sadan's roar. Many of the farm people stopped and looked up and around, staring into the skies. This was the first time that thunder was ever heard on earth.

Out in an open field, a group of young boys was learning archery, taught by Jaysha. She was showing her son, David, and his friends, how to aim correctly at the target. At the sound of Sadan's roar, the boys all stared up at the cloudy skies. David ran up to his mother.

"What was that, ma?"

"Fire magic going off at the celebration is my guess," replied Jaysha.

"It sounds like dragons!" exclaimed David, with excitement in his voice. While David and Jaysha talked, one of the young boys in the group started to goof around. Behind Jaysha's back, the young boy loaded an arrow and pointed it at another boy, making him cringe. The young boy then aimed the arrow straight up into the sky.

"I'll kill that dragon right now!"

The little boy let the arrow fly, and it disappeared quickly into the sky. Jaysha and David were still talking, unaware of the shot arrow. "I don't think that was a dragon; it was much too loud… and lasted much too long to be a dragon's roar. A dragon would have to be as big as a mountain to make a sound like that!" said Jaysha. Looking up towards the cloud, Jaysha whispered to herself "No way was that a dragon's roar… no way."

Meanwhile, the arrow was coming straight down, heading directly at David. The boy who shot the arrow warned the others, "Watch out!!!"

Jaysha looked at the young boy who yelled, noticing that he was looking directly up. Her eyes darted up to see what the boy was screaming about, and then screamed herself, "David!!!"

When the arrow was about ten feet directly above David, Jaysha instinctively shot out her arm and caught it only inches from David s head. "Whoa! David are you ok?"

A startled David nodded affirmatively.

"I don't know what I would do if I lost you too!"

With the arrow safely in Jaysha's hand, both mother and son were very relieved. While Jaysha hugged David, another young boy approached them.

"Did David's father really die fighting dragons?"

"No, of course, he didn't," replied Jaysha, surprised. "He's protecting the northern territory for our king."

"David said he died fighting dragons," the boy continued. "But everyone knows royal knights don't die!"

"Well, you know David… always making things bigger than life!" laughed Jaysha. "Like when he said he had a dragon for a friend!" Jaysha burst out, rubbing David's head.

"Yeah, we remember!!" responded the whole group of boys in unison. "That's right! We never did get to see your dragon friend, David," said one of David's friends.

"That's because the king ordered him dead! You…"

"That's it for today boys!" Jaysha interrupted. "We've certainly had enough fun with arrows for one day. Let's clean up!"

One of the young boys turned to David, "I'm gonna tell my dad you're a big liar!"

"Go and say anything you want to; David is just a great storyteller, that's all," Jaysha said, defending her son.

David looked at his mother, knowing that he was in big trouble.

Jaysha looked into her son's eyes and spoke softly.

"It's ok David. I've been waiting to tell someone the truth for a long time.

Your father deserves better than a secret funeral. These people should know he died protecting them!"

Jaysha gave David a big smile and a hug. Then they gathered up all the arrows from the practice lessons which Jaysha had been giving to make ends meet. Jaysha knew that all the young boys dreamed of being future royal knights and living forever.

In the late afternoon, the sky was still cloudy. Dagger and his clan of dragons had also been wondering what the loud sound was earlier.

"So it wasn't any of us that made the loud roaring sound?" asked Dagger. All the dragons shook their heads "no."

Dagger continued, "Well, if any of you think Merlinius will put up with us going against our agreement, you're wrong!"

"None of us did it!" protested Deetha.

Dagger decided to just drop the matter and lay down in a coiled position, quickly followed by the others. The dragons faded in and out of the heavy mist, seemingly sleeping on invisible beds.

When night came, stars sparkled all across the horizon in a beautiful panoramic scene, with a full moon brightly lighting up the clouds below. The reflection of the moonlight upon the clouds was like that of newly fallen snow.

The family of dragons led by Dagger gathered on top of the layer of clouds, and one by one, they went down inside the cloud.

Below the cloud line, the night is much darker as the clouds were blocking the moonlight of a full moon. Just below the clouds, the dragons began to appear one by one as they emerged from within the clouds.

Dagger and the other dragons descended, all the way to the ground.

As they touched the ground, they all spread out and began to eat from the abundant vegetation.

Elsewhere, Zindetha and his clan of dragons also descended from the clouds and down to the earth.

Fortunately, Zindetha, Deman, and the other meat-eating dragons landed at a different location from the plant eaters. They wanted to keep their existence a secret, and therefore they planned to stay as far away from Dagger and his clan as was possible.

Zindetha and the other meat eaters began looking around for something to eat. Deman saw a farm in the distance, and slowly and quietly crept up to the farmhouse, peeking inside one of the windows. The farmer's family sat at the dinner table while the mother carried a plate of roasted chicken to her husband and children. After serving the food, she sat down, and they began to eat. A giant eyeball belonging to Deman peered in the window. Looking behind him, he saw the silhouettes of the other dragons, each making a low growling noise.

Moving to the barnyard, several meat-eaters began tearing into and devouring penned up cows. A horse began to neigh profusely as the dragons continued feasting on the farmer's livestock. Unaware of what was happening outside, the family continued enjoying their meal.

Suddenly the father stopped chewing his food and listened intently to the tumult outside. He heard the sounds of his horses crying loudly and suddenly raised his hand.

"Stop talking son!" he demanded, listening as closely as he could. "Do any of you hear that?"

"Hear what, Daddy?" asked one of the children.

"I hear it, Daddy!" shouted another. "It's the horses!"

The farmer quickly stood and reached for a giant sword. He secured it and hastened to the door.

"Stay put until I get back!" he warned his family as he dashed out. Disregarding danger, he ran across the yard and around the corner toward the barn. Hurrying, as he heard his horses neigh louder, the farmer suddenly stopped as he saw several dragons completely devouring his livestock. The farmer froze in his tracks. Without notice,

Sadan's large head came down and seized the farmer's upper torso into his mouth, leaving the farmer's legs dangling from his mouth.

Sadan lifted his head upward, and with a couple of bites, the farmer was gone.

The mother and her children were fearfully huddled together in the back bedroom. Her body was tense and her palms sweaty, and with a trembling voice, she assured the children that they were safe. After a few hours, with the children fast asleep, the mother quietly slipped away, being ever so careful not to wake them. She went throughout the house checking for her husband.

The farmer's wife quietly called out to her husband, "Honey, where are you? Honey…" After receiving no response, she called louder, "Honey! Answer me, where are you?" Still getting no response, the wife cautiously walked outside the house and called for her husband again. "Daniel! Where are you!!?" She began to walk farther from the house, but thinking better of the idea, she quickly returned inside.

The sun shone brightly above the heavy cloud cover. Dagger and his family were playing amongst themselves, much like animals do, wrestling, and chasing one another. Rago eventually lost interest and became bored. He started looking around when suddenly his ears stood on end and twitched, as if listening to something. Rago then foolishly left the safety of his family. None of the adult dragons were paying attention and therefore did not notice that Rago had gone. Directly in front of Rago, a very faint shadow could be seen. It was barely visible, but it was there. Rago turned back and looked at his family.

Rago said to himself, "Hmm… everyone is over there?" He then turned back around, straining his eyes. "What is that?"

What Rago actually saw was Sadan's shadow! His mouth was drooling as he thought of the delight it would be to eat tender young dragon meat. But just as Sadan prepared to pounce, a roar was heard. It was Deetha, calling for her baby.

Deetha roared thunderously, "Rago! Come back here!"

"Oh no, I'm in trouble!" Rago said aloud as he quickly glided back to his mother, who was floating toward him. Sadan watched as Deetha floated over. "If that dragon had seen me, she would have had me for lunch!" Sadan said as he hurriedly turned around, flipping his tail out in the clear. Out of the corner of her eyes, Deetha caught a glimpse of Sadan's tail. She quickly raced to where Sadan had been but found nothing there.

"Hmm… what was that?" Deetha wondered. She then made her way back to where Rago was now waiting.

"I'm sorry, Mom," Rago whimpered. "I thought I saw something."

"So did I!" replied Deetha, now very confused.

Dagger floated over angrily to see what Rago had done now. "Rago, what did I tell you about—" Dagger began, before Deetha interrupted him.

"He saw something, and so did I," said Deetha.

"What are you talking about? Where?" asked Dagger.

"Out there," Deetha gestured.

Looking and seeing nothing, Dagger replied, "The clouds are just playing tricks on you two. I think I see things now and then too."

"No way, there was something out there," Deetha insisted.

"Well, it's not there now!" shouted Dagger impatiently. "Come on, let's get back with the others."

As Sadan glided along, he was ambushed by Zindetha, Deman, and the other meat eaters. They were furious at Sadan for getting too close and jeopardizing their secret existence. A fierce fight ensued, with the dragons so engaged in their fray that they disregarded the fact that they were exposing themselves by creating such a loud racket. Zindetha and Deman bit and clawed at Sadan while screaming curses at him.

"You almost were discovered, you fool!" Zindetha roared.

"How dare you put us in danger, we should kill you!" shouted Deman.

The fighting continued for a short while and then ended quickly as Sadan was whipped across the sky with a flick of Zindetha's mighty tail. Sadan roared in pain, and flames shot forth from his mouth. On earth, a few farmers looked up to hear thunder and see a bolt of lightning across the sky. They all muttered prayers as they peered heavenward. The loud sounds were heard by everyone this time. It was the second time that thunder was ever heard on earth.

Both King Arturus and Sir Solomon, who were sitting at a table, looked up and then around with complete amazement.

Jaysha and David were standing in front of their home, also looking up, wondering what they had just heard. "That was the same sound we heard earlier," said a confused David.

"It sure was. Hmm…" muttered Jaysha.

At his castle, even Merlinius was wondering what was happening. He stood out on his balcony peering up into the heavens in deep thought.

All the people in the kingdom were startled, quite terrified at the phenomenon they had just experienced. People began to huddle together. Horses were neighing and continuously bucking.

King Arturus came out from within his palace to the balcony, very confused and disturbed by the deafening sounds caused by the dragons in the clouds. However, his kingdom on the ground seemed normal.

The king saw Odious arrive down below at the front entrance of his castle. Seeing the Wizard's apprentice, King Arturus muttered to himself, "Merlinius is probably behind all this! But why does he send his student to do his dirty work?" The king turned and quickly went back inside his castle.

In the cloudy skies above, Dagger and the other plant eaters were gathered together.

"What was that, papa?" Rago asked his father. "What was that?" he asked again impatiently.

"I don't know," Dagger answered. "If I didn't know better, I'd say it sounded like dragons fighting, but it couldn't be!"

Sadan was at arms-length from Zindetha. But he was one angry dragon now.

"I am hungry…" said Sadan angrily. "I've never gone this long without eating!"

"I'm hungry too, but it's not worth risking us getting caught!" Zindetha replied, gritting his teeth. "Especially for a baby dragon which wouldn't fill us up anyway! We'll go down tonight and find a farmhouse with plenty of livestock."

Zindetha then turned away, feeling that dropping the matter, for now, was the best thing to do. All the meat-eating dragons drifted away into the safety of the clouds.

At dusk, in an Albion countryside, several gliding dragons touched the ground near a peaceful farmhouse. Sadan was leading the pack as they crept ever so cautiously to the farmhouse. The dragons surrounded the house. Strange sounds were coming from the dragons, sounds which became louder and louder until it resembled the sound of thunder.

Suddenly, screams of people in anguish pierced the night. Bright flashes radiated as a couple of bright strikes of electricity came shooting out from behind the farmhouse. One lightning strike hit a man and burned him up instantly, with yet another strike hitting trees, causing a fire. As dragon wings billowed and dragon roars thundered, it appeared like a storm was ravaging the land. When all the commotion eventually came to a stop, the dragons floated up and away as the fire continued to consume the once peaceful farmhouse.

Through the darkened sky, Deman and Zindetha ascended together to safety. They were now a much happier pair.

Pleased with what had happened, Deman said gleefully, "Burning the evidence was a good idea! Besides, men and cattle taste much better when cooked!"

"We must do what we have to to stay alive," Zindetha replied.

The dragons soared toward the clouds while the farmhouse below was engulfed in flames.

Chapter 7

In a castle conference room the next morning, King Arturus walked toward Sir Solomon, who was with another royal knight named Sir Jacob. Both knights bowed as the king approached.

"Rise, Solomon," King Arturus commanded solemnly. "I need you to bring Merlinius to me right away. The people are demanding answers, and I intend to give them some. That old man might have done something terrible."

"What do you mean?" asked Sir Solomon.

"Nothing," King Arturus replied. "Let's just say I might have a little insight."

"The people believe it is dragons, sire…" Sir Solomon said.

Angered by Sir Solomon's reply, King Arturus retorted, "Don't tell me what people are saying! I'm not deaf!! And why are you still here?"

"Forgive me, my king," Sir Solomon pleaded.

"Your command will be done!" Sir Solomon bowed, and both knights immediately exited the room.

Later that morning, Sir Solomon and Sir Jacob rode their horses at full gallop, following the same mountain trail which Dagger and his clan of dragons had taken to get to Merlinius' castle. Both riders jumped, one after another, over the collapsed part of the trail where Rago had fallen. The two knights continued onward toward the castle.

Merlinius was busy in his study, but from the corner of his eye, he noticed via one of his crystal balls that riders were coming. Merlinius glared into the ball to see who exactly was coming. Merlinius then drew the curtain closed to seal the magical crystal balls from sight, for their existence was a very closely guarded secret.

Arriving at the entrance of Merlinius' castle, Sir Solomon and Sir Jacob dismounted from their horses and proceeded to the door of the castle. Sir Solomon wasted no time announcing his arrival, banging on the door so loudly that his knocking could be heard throughout the castle. Merlinius hastily put something away and then quickly answered the door.

"I'm here to take you to the king," said Sir Solomon. "Unexplainable things are happening. The people of Albion are horrified; they're too afraid to go outside! No work is being done, no cattle being sold."

"So the king thinks I have the answers, does he?" Merlinius replied.

"Yes!" Sir Solomon responded adamantly. "The king does think you can tell him what is causing the deafening sound that makes the ground shake, the blinding lights in the sky, and a burned down farmhouse."

"The reason the king is concerned is if people won't go outside, then no work will get done and then no taxes will be paid!" Merlinius explained. "So tell me, do you think I should do as I'm told, like some beckoned servant?"

"I do think it would be wise," replied Sir Solomon.

Admiring Sir Solomon, Merlinius replied, "Wise huh!… Many say a wizard is wise! Well then, we better get going, we shan't keep the royal highness waiting for my wisdom any longer."

Sir Solomon was irritated at Merlinius' patronizing of the king, but he appreciated that the wizard was willing to do what was asked of him. He watched as Merlinius stowed a few things away. Then all three men hurriedly exited the castle. Both knights waited on their horses while Merlinius' apprentice saddled up his horse. Merlinius would generally have merely disappeared and traveled the easy way, but like all men of that era, he loved a good ride once in a while.

For some strange reason, Sir Solomon and Odious made eye contact, but nothing was said. Odious watched Merlinius as he and his escorts galloped away. It was evident by the look on Odious' face that he was up to something.

While the three men were on their way down the path, suddenly Merlinius vanished, leaving a galloping horse without a rider. When Sir Solomon turned to check on Merlinius, all he saw was an empty saddle. Both royal knights exchanged astonished looks and then looked around for Merlinius, who was nowhere in sight. Not knowing what else to do, the two knights continued on to King Arturus' castle.

Later that evening, a meeting took place inside a conference room in King Arturus' castle. The conference room was at full capacity, with lords, dukes, knights and even common townspeople in attendance. Some of the knights and town people were yelling loudly.

"I call this meeting to order!" King Arturus shouted. "I want everyone to calm down, or I'll have the place emptied! Jaysha are you here?" asked the king, looking around the room.

"Of course, I'm here, your goons made sure of that!" Jaysha replied disdainfully.

"Come forth," ordered King Arturus. "I'll overlook your disrespect this time, due to my own deep respect for your husband. But don't test me! I'll only tolerate so much. Understand?"

Jaysha eyeballed the royal knights, or 'goons' as she has just called them. It was clear that they were ready to pounce on her and drag her away.

"Yes, m'lord," Jaysha responded as respectfully as she could muster, given her contempt for the king. "Tis understood. May we talk about whatever that deafening sound was which came from the skies on the feast day?"

King Arturus answered, "Well, that is why we are all here, isn't it? I am actually pleased to inform the good people of Albion that I have received word concerning what it was that we have all been hearing. Now listen everyone! Merlinius is inventing new tools that will eventually benefit everyone. Unfortunately, some of his experiments have proven to be a bit too loud and… er, bright… somewhat explosive, in fact." The crowd rumbled with uneasiness.

King Arturus continued, "Grant you, they may have gone wrong. Terribly wrong. But Merlinius has given me his word that there is no cause for alarm for any of you."

"Why isn't Merlinius here now?" Jaysha queried. "Why isn't he telling us this? Where is he? And that doesn't explain why a woman's husband disappeared a few nights ago! I've also heard tell that Merlinius may be hiding dragons!" The townspeople became very uneasy again as she spoke these words.

Sir Solomon and Sir Jacob jumped down from their horses just as they came to a halt. A stable boy came to gather the horses. Both men proceeded to enter the castle when they heard a voice behind them.

"Going in without me?" Both men turn to see Merlinius.

"We figured you'd have come and gone by now," Sir Solomon answered. "Listen, the way you come and go is your business. I did my task when I informed you that your presence was requested!"

"Let's get on with it then," said Merlinius, gesturing toward the castle, which they then entered together.

Sir Solomon and Merlinius entered the still very crowded conference room. The first sight of Merlinius caused an uproar among the angry villagers. Cries of 'dragon lover' and 'sorcerer' were heard resounding throughout the spacious room.

The villagers continued to yell at Merlinius, "There he is! He's the cause of the disappearances and the torments from the sky!"

Fearing a riot, King Arturus loudly commanded, "Royal Knights! Lead the people out, this meeting is over!" While some knights hesitated, Sir Solomon further admonished them.

"You heard the king, everybody has to go!" Sir Solomon yelled. The royal knights immediately did as commanded. People were pushed out of the room, regardless of whether they were dukes, lords, or common villagers. Only King Arturus, Sir Solomon, a few other royal knights, and Merlinius were left in the conference room. The king turned to Merlinius.

"I have to apologize for the people, but they are greatly troubled by the recent events," said King Arturus.

Merlinius responded with concern, "I understand the people's angst completely. And quite honestly, I too, am distraught by what has taken place."

"Well, I took the liberty and told the people that the events witnessed here lately were experiments that you had performed which have gone wrong," King Arturus explained, pausing for effect. "And for the most part, I think they bought it."

"I don't buy it!" shouted Jaysha, appearing from behind a wall where she had hidden during the evacuation of the conference room. "I don't buy any of it! The farmer went missing from his house, nowhere near Merlinius' castle." She stood defiantly looking at the king after her unfriendly utterance. Everyone in the room was stunned by her boldness.

Sir Solomon cautioned her, "Jaysha! You must…"

"No! Let her speak," interrupted Merlinius.

"A farmer's wife said she found blood on the ground the morning after her husband had disappeared," Jaysha stated.

"This is the first I've heard of this!" Merlinius replied.

Jaysha continued, furious with Merlinius reply, "Don't tell us you don't know! I have heard that your apprentice has proof that you're behind everything that is going on, old man!"

"You're way out of line!" Sir Solomon yelled at Jaysha.

Merlinius' eyes glowed with resentment, but he knew Jaysha's suspicions were justified.

"Settle down everyone!" King Arturus ordered. "I'm sure Merlinius will do what he has to. And I'll get to the truth. Besides, Odious only accused Merlinius of hiding dragons. He had no proof. Sir Jacob, bring me the papers Odious brought which described a spell of some kind."

Sir Jacob left the room. While everyone awaited the royal knight's return, Merlinius was feeling the heat, a very unusual feeling for him. "I can't wait," said Merlinius. "I have to go find Odious and confront him face to face about his accusations. I believe he has done a terrible deed!"

As Merlinius started to leave, Sir Solomon approached the king and said, "Your Majesty, I would like to ask Merlinius some questions before he leaves."

"Be quick about it."

Both men turned toward Merlinius, but he had pulled the disappearing act and was gone. Sir Solomon and King Arturus simply looked at each other.

The moon was almost full, as seen through a pocket of clearing within the clouds. The clan of the plant-eating dragons was waiting to go down for a food excursion. Rago glided over to his mother.

"Mom, I have an awful feeling that something bad is coming," Rago said.

"Don't worry son, your father will protect us," Deetha replied.

"What's taking him so long to come back?" asked Rago.

"He had a lot to go do, Rago," Deetha responded. "Your father should be back anytime. Just try to be patient."

Rago saw that an object was coming toward him. As the object came closer, it became apparent that it was his father returning from his trip.

"What took so long?" asked Deetha, relieved to see him. "You were gone for three days!"

"Merlinius caged me!" he shouted. "He said he had to, but then, something changed his mind, and he let me go."

"What are you talking about?" asked Deetha.

"I'm telling you Merlinius caged me!" Dagger continued. "Villagers have been vanishing and even Merlinius doesn't know why. Plus King Arturus is suspicious that Merlinius has done something behind his back. He also suspects that it's dragons causing the disappearances of some villagers."

"Oh no, we're doomed!" Deetha cried.

"Well, right now Merlinius is trying to find out what's actually causing the disappearances," said Dagger.

"He doesn't think it's us?" Deetha questioned. "We eat plants!"

"Merlinius wouldn't say," Dagger said. "But at least he let me go."

The rest of the other dragons all gathered around to listen as Dagger continued, "Everyone, the moon is giving off enough light to find plenty of food. Strange things have been happening, so everyone be careful! And do not, I repeat, do not let any human see you!" The dragons then descended one by one to the earth's surface.

The dragons took their time filling their bellies. Rago had grown bored, as children often do, and began wandering away from his family of dragons. Rago wrestled and growled at bushes as he made his way through them. The bushes came to an end, causing Rago to stop and look up, seeing a farmhouse located at the far end of a meadow.

"That's where David lives!" Rago said with excitement.

The young dragon broke into a full sprint all the way across the meadow, quickly coming to a stop in front of the farmhouse. Rago sneaked around the house and stopped just below an open window.

Underneath the window was broken boards which were once used as shutters. Rago looked into the open window.

"Yep, this is it," Rago said quietly to himself. "David's room. I broke these boards sneaking David out one night."

From within the open window, all that could be seen outside were dark forest and stars in the background. Suddenly, two claws came over the window frame, grabbing hold firmly. Seconds later, Rago's big face popped up. Barely hanging on by his claws, Rago looked in and saw his long-lost friend in bed sleeping.

Rago whispered, growling, "David… David." Getting no response, he spoke a little louder, "David… it's me… Rago!"

Becoming very anxious, Rago spat a gooey substance inside the room which hit the sleeping David right in the face. David quickly sat up in his bed.

"Rago!" David yelled joyfully wiping the sticky goo off his face.

Rago fell back outside from the windowsill just as David's mother came running into his room. Thinking quickly, David pretended that he had just awakened from a bad dream.

"Mom!" exclaimed David, startled. "I just dreamed my dragon friend was being killed right in front of me! It was so horrible!"

"Shhh… it will be okay," Jaysha replied.

David acted like he was quickly falling back to sleep. Jaysha gently put him under the blanket. But in doing so, she discovered the gooey stuff which the baby dragon spat earlier.

"Ugh… what is this stuff?" Jaysha whispered to herself. She thought momentarily about waking David but decided against it. "I'll deal with it tomorrow," she said, as she got up to leave. "It wouldn't be normal not to find weird stuff in David's room," she laughed as she walked out. After his mom closed the door, David immediately jumped up and ran to the window.

"Rago!… Rago!!" David called to his long-lost friend. Rago surprised David by springing up from under the window and licking his face as a pet dog would. Rago then jumped back down to the ground outside. David, with his upper torso out of the window, began moving his arms and hands while talking to Rago, again communicating by some kind of sign language.

"Rago! It's really you! I hoped I'd be able to see you again."

Rago communicated with David by using sign language of his own, bobbing his head up, down and then sideways.

David repeated what Rago just told him, "You have to go?… Why? Will you come back?"

Rago informed his friend that he would indeed return. "When?" David asked.

David watched closely as his dragon friend informed him he would return tomorrow.

Rago scampered off as David watched. He climbed back into his bed smiling, happy that his little friend Rago hadn't been killed as he had thought. David whispered to himself, "I knew you wouldn't let them get you, Rago!" With a smile on his face, he drifted off to sleep.

Meanwhile, in the forest, the family of plant-eating dragons finished eating for the night. Deetha looked over and saw her son Rago coming out of the bushes, eating gobs of plants. Rago looked back at his mother. Knowing that it was time to go, he gobbled as much as he could. Deetha turned back around, happy in knowing that her little Rago was safe. The family of dragons was generally having a good time on this particular night. One of them, named Racus, laughed aloud.

"Good thing we're weightless!" Racus said jokingly. "No way would we be able to even walk, much less fly after eating so much!"

As the family of plant-eating dragons ascended, they vanished one by one into the clouds.

Zindetha and the other meat-eating dragons came out from behind some thick plant growth nearby where the family of plant eaters had been moments earlier. It was from there that the meat eaters had been spying on the plant- eating dragons.

"Did any of you see where the young dragon went?" Zindetha asked.

"I saw him come back from over there," Deman said, turning his head and pointing to where the trees started to thin out. They all walked towards the thinning trees until a light was seen somewhere beyond the trees.

Zindetha came to a clearing and stopped at the beginning of a meadow. He could see Jaysha and David's farmhouse, with the glowing light of a candle in the window.

"What are we waiting for?" Sadan asked suddenly. "Let's go get us some cows, pigs… and humans!" he added devilishly.

"Nah, aren't you still full from the mammoth we just took down?" Zindetha asked. "Let's come back here tomorrow." The pack of meat-eating dragons soared up to the clouds.

The following afternoon, Rago was playing, as he had been doing all day happily, along with the other dragons. He was having an especially good time, probably in part because he planned to visit his friend when they went back down to eat later that night. Deetha observed how much fun Rago was having and wondered aloud, "What has gotten into him?" She then glided over and stopped Rago in his tracks. Rago looked up at her in puzzlement.

"What have you been up to?" Deetha asked. "Last night you disappeared for quite a while, didn't you?"

"No mother… I was right by you the whole time," Rago protested.

"You better have been, little one," Deetha replied.

"Of course, mother," Rago said, with puppy-like eyes.

Night time came quickly to Albion, but not soon enough for Rago. The families of dragons came out from within the clouds with

Rago out in front, gliding as he led the way for his family as they all descended from the clouds.

That night, as a full moon hovered over the forest, the family of plant- eating dragons touched the ground and quickly started chowing down. Rago slowly snuck away under the pretense of gobbling up more plant food. Rago turned to look at his family to make certain they hadn't noticed that he was a good distance away. As soon as he dared, Rago ducked behind some bushes and darted off into the forest, running across a meadow toward David's farmhouse.

At the house, David was leaning out of his bedroom window. On this beautiful night, well-lit from the full moon above, David could see Rago running toward him from across the meadow.

"Rago!" David yelled, happy to see his friend. David automatically jumped out of the window and ran to greet his friend. Rago once again licked David's face as a dog would, and they both headed off toward the forest. They walked and played together until both came to a halt. "We used to have so much fun, Rago," said David. "I hope nobody finds out about you." Rago's head moved up and down vigorously. "Rago, is your family alive?" Rago nodded.

"Where are they?" asked David, understandably surprised. Rago communicated his answer via the usual sign language, prompting David to respond, "You can't tell me? It's a secret? I understand. You have to keep them safe." David and Rago continued their walk until they eventually reached the end of the meadow. Without hesitation they both advanced, disappearing among the trees.

Then they relaxed a bit. David rested, leaning back on a rock. Rago knew he would get in big trouble if he didn't get back to his family soon. Rago communicated this news to a disappointed David. "You have to say goodbye? So soon?" David asked dejectedly.

Rago nodded.

As they were saying goodbye, they suddenly heard something which made them freeze where they stood. The sound they heard continually grew louder and seemed to be coming their way. They both ducked into high weeds for cover.

Three dragons came out from beyond some trees, making a low rumbling sound. At first, Rago thought the three dragons were part of his family and started silently signaling to David.

"It's your parents looking for you," David said, turning around as the three dragons came closer. Suddenly, Rago frantically turned to David and fired out a warning signal. A surprised David responded, "What? They're not your parents?"

The dragons were grumbling loud enough for Rago to make out what they were saying. Rago turned to David and relayed more information.

"They're going to go eat cows and pigs?" David queried.

Rago did not answer because the dragons were almost upon them. They both dropped down as deeply as possible into the high weeds. The three dragons passed over David and Rago, but, miraculously, did not see them. One dragon's colossal claw foot almost crushed David as he passed by. Rago could hear the dragons also talking about eating humans. The three meat- eating dragons were so fixated on their mission at hand that they were oblivious to the chance of having Rago and David as appetizers.

After the dragons passed, David and Rago got up and stealthily followed them as they reached the meadow. As the dragons continued across the meadow, Rago quickly realized what the three dragons were planning to do. Wasting no time, Rago turned and relayed his concerns to David.

"They're going to eat my mother?" David responded, horrified. "Rago, do something! Anything!"

Rago immediately roared as loud as he could!

Zindetha, Deman, and Sadan all stopped in their tracks and quickly turned to see which one of them had fallen behind and was now calling out. Much to their surprise, they realized that the roar had not come from any of them.

"Look!" Deman said in a panicked voice. "It's that little dragon. And he's with a human!"

"What are you fools waiting for?" Zindetha yelled. "Go get them! Don't let them get away!"

David and Rago took off for cover in the thick forest. Deman and Sadan scrambled and took flight after their prey. David and Rago split up and ran in different directions. Deman and Sadan crisscrossed in their pursuit and then violently crashed into each other. Zindetha roared in disgust. She looked back longingly at the farmhouse but decided that the best course was to go help capture Rago and David. Zindetha zoomed off, soaring just feet above the ground in hot pursuit. At the farmhouse, Jaysha heard the thunderous roars. She immediately ran to check on her son but discovered that he was gone. Dashing to David's open window, she could faintly see dragons at the far end of the meadow. A flush of panic swept through Jaysha's body, for her beloved boy was nowhere in sight. Jaysha dashed back into the hallway and raced out of her house in full sprint, yelling as she ran.

"David! Where are you?" she screamed as loudly as she could. "David!" Jaysha ran across the yard and into the barn. Just moments later, Jaysha emerged from the barn on her horse, with her bow in hand. After taking one last look around for her son, she kicked her horse into a full gallop. Fearless, she headed in the direction where she had just seen the dragons.

Deman was closing in fast on Rago. Zindetha was also gaining ground. As Deman made ready to pounce on Rago, he laughed viciously.

"You're mine this time!" Deman growled, mouth salivating.

Out of nowhere, Rago's father, Dagger, intercepted Deman. He hit him head-on, knocking him down with tremendous force. Deman tumbled out of control, crushing down trees as he went. Dagger had rescued his son, for the moment anyway. Zindetha, seeing what had happened, darted off into the darkness.

Meanwhile, David, who was being chased by Sadan, was about to be captured. David's face showed terror as he frantically looked for some way to escape. His eyes grew twice as big when he saw a hole in the side of a ravine. Without hesitation, David dove right into it.

Just then, Sadan's claw swiped across the hole and barely missed David as he burrowed in deeper. Sadan began furiously digging out the hole in which David had taken refuge.

By now Dagger and Deman were engaged in a fierce battle. The force being caused by the furious flapping of their wings caused them to spin upward into the skies, faster and faster. Clashing out of control, the fierceness of their battle stirred the wind up into a force the likes of which had never been seen before. Their tails were also moving the wind with such force that they created funnel-shaped clouds.

CHAPTER 8

In the study of his castle that night, Merlinius was watching through one of the crystal balls as the fierce battle between Dagger and Deman unfolded. The crystal ball showed the two dragons spinning out of control as they continued battling. The spinning dragons appeared like a funnel of swirling clouds connecting the skies to the ground. Even Merlinius seemed to be in shock as he took a closer look at the first tornado ever to happen. He could see a villager's dwelling being ripped apart as the tornado moved about on the ground. The dragon-made tornado continued until it caused severe damage to an entire village.

In the forest wilderness, Deetha was soaring right above the tree line, looking for Rago. She finally spotted him and glided over and landed next to Rago.

"Son, are you all right!?" Deetha asked, relieved to find him. "Yeah, I'm sorry Ma, but there's a human in trouble!"

"There's a what?" Deetha queried.

"Ma, I'll tell you later!" Rago shouted, looking for David. "Right now we have to go and help him!" Rago raced off in the direction of the commotion Sadan was making. Sadan continued frantically digging away in his efforts to get to David. David's clothes were being snagged and torn by Sadan's massive claws.

As Rago and Deetha soared just above the trees, Rago was the first one to see Sadan digging away.

"Look! There he is!" Rago yelled.

"Where?" Deetha asked her son.

"Over there!" Rago said, pointing in the direction of Sadan.

"I'll go! Wait here," Deetha told Rago. Deetha spotted her target, tucked in her wings and went into a nose dive. David was screaming bloody murder while kicking at Sadan's claws.

"Help! Help me! Somebody help me! Ahhhh!!!"

David was scared stiff, his eyes wide open. It appeared that David was a goner. Sadan raised his massive claw to strike the deadly blow, but just as his claw started to swing down, Deetha blindsided him, knocking him onto his back. Sadan frantically got up and immediately soared up into the sky. Deetha, wasting no time, gave chase.

David, seeing that it was now safe to come out of his hiding place, climbed out and ran into the darkness of the forest. In the full moonlight, Sadan quickly made it into the cover of the clouds, but Deetha caught him anyway. The two began to engage in a fierce battle as well. Both Deetha and Sadan started blowing fire strike after fire strike at each other.

Down on the ground, the fire strikes from the dragons fighting above appeared like lightning bolts, and the noise of the dragon roars sounded like thunder. As the fight continued, the roiling clouds continually darkened, and rain began to slash around the fighting dragons. This was actually the first thunderstorm ever recorded in history.

In the sky not too far away, Deman and Dagger continued their fight. Zindetha seemingly came out from nowhere and joined in to help defeat Dagger. Zindetha roared as she joined the battle. The roaring thunder of the dragons fighting grew even louder as Dagger got help of his own when Racus came to his aid. The battle was out of control, with all four dragons biting, clawing, and blowing fire.

Deetha had freed herself from entanglement with Sadan and was now dodging fire strike after fire strike. Suddenly, one of the plant-eating dragons ascended to help Deetha fight Sadan.

In the forest near the village, the blown fire strikes appeared as lightning bolts coming down and randomly striking the ground. Numerous people were now watching the phenomenon of lightning and thunder take place. It was also now raining hard on the ground.

The battle above raged on, resulting in continual thunder and lightning with no let-up. A tree, struck by lightning, caught fire. A villager, standing too close to a lightning strike, fell backward, completely stunned.

Many other villagers were hiding from the lightning and thunder in their homes. People huddled and cringed each time the thunder vibrated throughout their houses. Horses, cattle, and dogs were going mad with the sounds and lights. Cats and mice scurried for shelter. Forgetting their usual hostility, a cat and mouse were seen beneath a bed, cuddled together in fright. At King Arturus' castle, all could be seen by the full moon that night. The battle up above was peaking, with lightning cracking across the sky, and thunder so loud that eardrums were ringing. King Arturus and his royal knights were hastily getting their armor on. King Arturus entered the conference room. Sir Solomon was there waiting for him in full armor.

"Your Majesty, the battle of all battles has begun!" shouted Sir Solomon. "Your armies of knights are waiting for orders!"

"We appear to be under attack," replied King Arturus. "Are there many casualties?"

"No, so far no deaths have been reported," Sir Solomon responded.

"Well, that's good!" King Arturus exclaimed. "Let's mount up and go take a look for ourselves!"

"Right away, Your Majesty!" Sir Solomon answered.

In Merlinius' castle, the wizard was still watching intently as everything was unfolding through the crystal ball. Watching the dragons battle in the clouds, he observed them blowing fire of lightning bolt after lightning bolt at each other. Merlinius could see the lightning bolts striking the ground, striking the trees, and striking the farmhouses. Merlinius noticed Rago, the young dragon, waiting alone. Suddenly a human, a young boy, came running up to Rago. Merlinius was now even in more shock.

"What in the world is happening?" Merlinius exclaimed. He then vanished into a puff of sparkles.

As soon as David joined Rago, he began asking questions.

"What in the world is going on, Rago?" David asked. Rago frantically signed back to David, inquiring as to how the young boy had escaped the dragon's clutches.

"How did I get away?" David responded. "I saw a small cave and dove right into it! Barely made it too! Then out of nowhere another dragon came and started fighting with the one that was digging me out for his dinner!"

Rago is almost dancing as he signed to his friend, *That was my mother who saved your life! Merlinius sent our family to go live up in the clouds…*

"How did he manage that?" David asked.

Rago replied, *He made my entire family weightless.*

"Wow!" responded David. "So, what are those ear deafening booms coming from the skies? And the fire that is brighter than the sun? Is all that coming from dragons?"

I think so, Rago answered.

"So, there must be more dragons in the clouds besides your family? Did Merlinius send other dragons up to the clouds?"

I don't know, Rago answered, puzzled.

"We have to go and find Merlinius!" shouted David. "He can tell us what is happening!"

Rago agreed, and the two of them went running off into the darkness.

Jaysha continued to search in vain for her son. She brought her galloping horse to a halt and moved the steed around in circles as she called, "David, David!" After a short pause and with no response from David, Jaysha bucked her horse into a gallop in the opposite direction from which David and Rago had just gone.

In the sky that night, the battle raged on, with the full moon as a backdrop. A dragon wildly sprayed fire, causing massive strikes of lightning to shoot across the sky.

Lightning bolts continued hitting village dwellings, causing numerous fires, but fortunately, the rain quickly doused most of them. People could still be seen running out from burning houses. Total chaos had taken over with cattle, horses, pigs, and chickens running wildly with the people.

The king and his posse of royal knights were riding on their horses through the darkness. A couple of them were carrying burning torches as they all rode on. A blazing fire could be seen burning through the trees. As the posse came closer, the riders could see several dwellings of a small village ablaze. Sir Solomon yelled out, "Sire! Yonder, a village burns!"

The king and his posse all spurred their horses to run faster, so they could give aid to the villagers attempting to put out the fires. King Arturus stayed saddled, as the royal knights dismounted and aided the villagers. Meantime, Sir Solomon was riding his horse from one end to the other of the smoldering village. Sir Solomon approached the king.

"Sire, I've searched everywhere! No traces of the enemy can be found!"

In the sky, the battle between the dragons was wearing down, as one of the meat eaters was getting severely beaten. The beaten dragon finally made a break-away and took off for cover into denser, thicker clouds. Another meat- eater, who was also getting beat, followed suit and ran for protection as well. His opponent, a plant eater, gave chase.

The electrical storm caused by the fighting dragons was moving eastward as the plant eaters continued their pursuit of the meat eaters. The pursuing dragons quickly came to a stop when Dagger shouted out to his clan.

"They are nothing but cowards! Let's go back; we might get ambushed!" Dagger shouted, as he and his clan turned around and flew back.

In the forest, Merlinius appeared from thin air right in front of David and Rago, causing them to bump into him. David and Rago were both delighted to see Merlinius.

"Where do you two think you're going?" Merlinius asked.

"We were on our way to see you!" David answered abruptly. Rago began to converse with Merlinius through telepathy.

"My parents are fighting evil meat eaters up in the clouds!" Rago exclaimed.

"The skies are filled with fire and sounds so loud, it nearly breaks your eardrums!" David shouted.

"Yes, I have seen these things too," Merlinius replied. "You both must come with me, you'll be safer." Merlinius grabbed hold of David and Rago and then, with a blink of an eye, all three vanished.

At the burning village that night, as the driving rain abated, King Arturus watched as the royal knights and villagers formed single file lines, passing buckets of water over to burning structures. He watched admiringly as his royal knights and the townspeople did a remarkable job of extinguishing the last of the fires in the village.

After all the fires were extinguished, the king, with some royal knights and townspeople, began discussing what they had just witnessed.

"So, no one here saw who caused all the fires?" King Arturus asked, astounded.

"No one, Your Majesty!" responded one of the villagers. "We're telling you, the fire came from the sky. Except it wasn't fire, it was like the sun itself came down and struck the land!"

"I'd say it was more like thunderous bolts of heavenly light!" another villager said. "It has to be an attack of some kind. For right after the bolt would hit, a loud booming sound would follow!"

"Perhaps our longtime enemies to the north have new weapons and are staging a surprise attack," Sir Solomon surmised.

"We have been at peace with the Thuringians for years," King Arturus said. "I can't believe they would ruin what we have worked so long for."

Jaysha, her horse at full gallop, came riding into the village. She quickly dismounted, even before her horse came to a complete halt, right in front of the king.

"King Arturus!" Jaysha shouted, trying to catch her breath. "My son is missing. I fear dragons have gotten him!"

"Slow down, lady Jaysha," King Arturus responded. "Did you say dragons? Are you sure, woman?"

"Yes! I've seen them with my own eyes!" Jaysha replied, breathing hard.

"They also had something, a force... I have never seen before!
From their mouths, they now blow fire brighter than the sun!"

"That would explain the blinding fire coming from the sky," Sir Solomon responded. "Sire, Merlinius must be behind this; his apprentice was telling us the truth."

"Yes, that appears to be the case," King Arturus replied. "Sir Solomon, get the men ready to ride out. We're going to pay Merlinius a visit. I'm interested in seeing how that old wizard is going to explain this."

The king and his knights took off, kicking their horses into a full gallop. Jaysha had now joined them. They galloped through the forest as fast as their horses could carry them.

Deetha touched down on the ground and started to frantically look for Rago. "Rago!" Deetha yelled. "Where are you? Rago, Rago!"

Racus, one of the plant eaters, came down and landed next to Deetha. "Racus, I can't find my Rago anywhere!" Deetha continued, fearing her son might be dead.

"Don't worry! He has probably found cover somewhere," Racus reassured her. "We'll find him." The two dragons quickly started searching the area for Rago.

The rest of the family of plant eaters, including Dagger, touched ground one at a time. Deetha ran over to tell Rago's father the dreaded news.

"Our baby's gone," moaned Deetha in despair.

"We must go to Merlinius," suggested Dagger. "He will be able to find our son. Racus, you and the others follow, but circle Merlinius' castle high above, hidden in the clouds." The family of dragons all flew away toward the ominous mountain range.

Merlinius, David, and Rago appeared out of thin air in the castle's study. Merlinius quickly walked over and grabbed one of the crystal balls. He then gestured to David and Rago to follow him as he exited the study. They walked down a hallway and then turned into an open doorway.

Merlinius began arranging luminescent jars in order as if preparing to cast some spell. David and Rago were looking all around with fascination at all of the fantastical things Merlinius had in the laboratory.

"Wow, talk about having toys!" David said, amazed.

Up above Dagger and Deetha, Zindetha had been following close behind the family of plant eaters. Zindetha watched as Dagger and Deetha touched ground just in front of Merlinius' castle. She was surprised to see that, instead of landing as well, the other plant-eating dragons soared yet higher into the clouds.

Zindetha landed in a crevice on the mountainside and hid within It. She could see Deetha and Dagger begin to make a ruckus in front of Merlinius' castle.

Dagger roared with all his might. "LET US IN! MERLINIUS! WE NEED YOUR HELP!"

CHAPTER 9

Merlinius heard Dagger's roars and hastily walked over to a lever mounted on a wall. Merlinius quickly pulled the lever, causing the wall to roll open exposing the outside environment. Merlinius looked over the edge and saw Dagger and Deetha looking up. Merlinius hastily gestured for them to come up. Immediately, both dragons did as commanded.

Rago's parents floated through the opened wall and then touched ground next to their son. Dagger's face, upon seeing Rago, showed a range of emotions, first surprise, then relief, and then pure joy. Rago's reuniting with his parents was a very touching moment, but as parents do, Dagger felt a need for discipline as well.

"Rago! Why didn't you stay close to us?" Dagger growled. "You were almost killed tonight! Don't you understand how dangerous it can be by yourself? The king's men…"

"Don't be mad!" David interrupted, looking up to Dagger. "Your son saved my mother from dragons that were going to eat her! He's a hero!"

Dagger looked frustrated.

Merlinius then stated, "He's telling the truth, Dagger. Rago has shown great bravery for such a young life. Be proud of your son!"

Rago stood next to David, both of them watching as Merlinius and Dagger conversed.

His father and Merlinius were discussing different possibilities as to how they could bring an end to the meat eaters while sparing the lives of the plant eaters. Merlinius knew that, as long as the meat-eating dragons existed, there would never be peace on earth.

As Merlinius and Dagger continued to talk, Odious peeked through the crack of an open door. "What is it you're going to do now, you old snake?" Odious whispered to himself. "Oh, how I wish the king were here now to see for himself that you are the betrayer."

Odious snuck away down the hallway and out a side door of the castle, quickly hopping on his horse and galloping away.

Zindetha could see that Odious was coming right towards him. Just as Odious was approaching Zindetha's hiding place, Zindetha jumped out, causing Odious to fall from his horse and tumble to the ground. Odious rolled entirely off the path and over the vertical cliff, but Zindetha snagged him with her claw and pulled him back, pinning Odious down. Zindetha's razor- sharp claw pressed down on Odious' chest, while her razor-sharp teeth drooled with delight.

"What's the hurry? What's going on in there? What's the old man up to now?" Zindetha questioned Odious anxiously.

Odious was very frightened and stuttered his reply, "Merlinius is about to perform another spell of some kind… and there is also a young boy with them. I have to get the king and bring him here so he can see for himself that Merlinius betrayed the decree of the kingdom."

"The kingdom's evil decree to eradicate my kind!" Zindetha barked, raising her head in thought. "That young boy must be the one that saw us! I can't let him tell the king that dragons are still alive… I must get him. But how? Hmmm…" He lowered his head for a face to face with Odious and continued, "Listen, human, I know of a weakness Merlinius has! Bring me the young human boy, and I'll tell you what that weakness is. … You could replace Merlinius and become the king's own wizard! That would suit you, yes?"

Odious was suspicious of Zindetha; her words sounded hollow. "You think I can trust you? After trying to eat me? How brazenly stupid can you be?!"

"What's stopping me from eating you now?" Zindetha mocked, showing her pearly whites. "Ha! You wouldn't be much more than a snack… and a tough little bony snack at that! Listen, you runt. Right now, neither of us have a choice!"

"Merlinius and I are probably finished anyway," said Odious, as a million thoughts were going through his mind. "You're right, we don't have a choice. I'll do it."

Zindetha drew his face even closer to Odious' face, teeth dripping with saliva.

"Merlinius' weakness is…" Zendetha paused, thinking, not sure if he should tell but finally, he continued. "His power is useless without his wand. Now get me the kid! And you better not fail, human… or we're both doomed!" Zindetha finally released Odious and immediately flew off into the clouds, nearly blowing Odious off the cliff with the force of her mighty wings.

Odious opened the same side door he came out of earlier and vindictively shouted, "My time is almost here. Merlinius, it may be time for you to retire." Odious then went inside the castle.

Merlinius was still talking things over with Dagger. David continued looking around amazed at all the different scientific things in Merlinius' laboratory.

"Dagger, you have to gather your entire family and be here before sunrise," Merlinius said.

"We'll be here!" Dagger responded as he went over to Deetha and Rago. Odious, who had crept up to the laboratory to lay in wait, hid and listened.

As David took a closer look at Merlinius' several crystal balls, He noticed that something was in one of them.

"The king and his knights are coming!" David shouted, startling everyone.

Then, turning to look closer into the crystal ball, "My mother is with them!"

Merlinius quickly came over to verify what David had just stated. He saw that the king and his knights were indeed coming and were just reaching the start of the incline of the mountain path.

"Dagger!" Merlinius shouted. "You and your family must flee at once! The king must not see you!"

Dagger gave a nod of agreement and then quickly gestured for Deetha and son to follow. Deetha and Rago hastily followed Dagger; all three moving toward the opened wall. The three dragons flew away, heading toward higher mountains where peaks lay hidden in clouds that were reflecting the radiant colors of dawn. Merlinius began making preparations for a magic spell.

As dawn arrived, Odious was watching Merlinius making the preparations for the spell through a narrow crack between the slightly opened door of the corridor.

"If I clobber the old man over the head, getting the kid will be a cinch," Odious whispered to himself. "What irony. This kid is the son of that pompous knight, Sir Jonathan, who Zindetha ate. Now, Zindetha can have his son for dessert."

Odious opened the door and quietly started moving toward Merlinius who didn't suspect a thing. Odious could see that David was staring into a crystal ball, engulfed, watching his mother riding her horse at full gallop.

Up above in the sky, Zindetha had already joined up with the other meat eaters. They split up and began going in different directions, creeping up to Merlinius' castle and taking various positions around the fortress.

Odious was behind a cabinet stacked with different kinds of jars filled with luminescent powders. Odious saw a mallet nearby and quietly picked it up.

Odious crept within striking distance and raised the mallet to strike Merlinius, thinking to himself, *Time to take you out, old man!*

Merlinius, who was just beginning a magic spell, swung around his magical wand, oblivious that Odious was about to kill him. From the corner of David's eyes, he saw what Odious was about to do.

"Merlinius, watch out!" David yelled. David jumped up and accidentally knocked over a crystal ball, causing it to fall to the floor and burst open.

Merlinius dipped to the side and dodged most of Odious' swing, but the mallet nicked Merlinius, causing him to stumble and fall onto some nearby tables which had luminescent jars on them. Jars were now breaking and spilling onto the floor, Mixing together all kinds of magical ingredients with other mysterious things: animal claws, different colored crystals, even a couple of eyeballs.

An energy source of some kind began to form as the result of the unexpected mix of magical ingredients and the broken crystal ball. The swirling pool of energy of colors created by the spillage grew wider and wider.

Chapter 10

Rago was still traveling upward with his parents to avoid detection by King Arturus and his knights when his ears suddenly stood on end as he heard the yells of his friend David below. Fearing that his friend was in danger, he made an about turn and made a beeline back to Merlinius' castle.

Inside the castle, Odious continued swinging the mallet at Merlinius who, for an older man, was really quite agile. In fact, he appeared to be easily dodging each swing. Then with one swing of Merlinius' wand, the mallet went flying out of Odious' hand and landed across the room. The two wizards were engaged in a pretty good struggle, with very much at stake.

David watched as Merlinius and Odious fought. He so wanted to help his friend Merlinius. He noticed the bright growing body of light caused by the spillage. David looked directly at the energy and saw a swirling pool of colors that seemed to be tearing apart and swallowing up the wooden floor as it continued to grow wider. The amorphous blob of colors swallowed up the laboratory floor.

Outside the castle, Zindetha was watching, when she suddenly noticed something beginning to fly down from high above. The small dot Zindetha had noticed was now getting bigger and bigger.

Zindetha eyed the object and soon realized that it was Rago who was approaching the castle. Rago, returning to help his friend, descended near where the meat eaters were hiding. Zindetha watched as Rago came closer, about to pass right over her. Zindetha prepared to leap.

"I'm finally gonna get you, just a little closer…" Zindetha said, drooling. As Rago flew over, Zindetha lunged at him but missed. Rago barely felt one of Zindetha's claws, and then darted and swooped away.

Inside the laboratory, the two wizards were still battling. David was startled by a loud crashing sound made by a large cabinet that Merlinius magically sent flying toward Odious.

Odious ducked and scrambled behind some knocked over tables, causing Merlinius to momentarily lose track of him.

"Where are you? You coward!" shouted Merlinius.

Odious jumped up and threw a crystal rock at Merlinius, hitting him in the head.

Merlinius screamed in pain as he fell hard to the floor. Dropping his Magic Wand David, seeing that Merlinius had taken a severe hit, immediately went to him to help him get back on his feet.

Odious using Magic of his own, retrieves the mallet he had lost earlier by simply having it fly into his hands. Seeing David helping Merlinius, Odious went after him to try to scare him off. But brave David didn't run. Instead, he started throwing bottles at Odious. While many of the bottles hit the wall behind Odious, some hit their mark, slowing Odious down considerably.

Outside, in the sky, Zindetha was in hot pursuit of Rago and was gaining ground, getting closer and closer. Zindetha thrust her large wings harder and harder as he zeroed in on Rago. His eyes grew bigger with excitement as he was almost upon his target.

Rago, seemingly running out of gas, began to slow down. Zindetha could almost taste his breakfast, his mouth watering with anticipation. Suddenly, Rago veered downward toward Merlinius' castle, tucking his wings for maximum speed. Zindetha was angered by this unexpected burst of Rago's pure will to survive, helping him to streak downward at incredible speed.

"You can't get away!" Zindetha roared, as he also tucked his wings for maximum speed downward. Once again, he started to close in on Rago, this time at a much faster rate.

Rago swiftly changed direction in hopes of eluding his capture. Rago was now heading straight for the castle, while Zindetha, oblivious to his direction of flight, is focused entirely on Rago. Zindetha failed to realize that he was headed straight for the castle wall.

Rago spied a small porthole, difficult to see, but possibly big enough for Rago to fit through. The smaller dragon soared in the direction of the small porthole.

Zindetha, still oblivious that he was headed for the wall, followed in full pursuit of Rago. At the last minute, Rago tucked his wings as tight as he could and shot right through the castle porthole. But foolish Zindetha, like a runaway train, collided horribly into the castle wall. The crash brought boulder-sized bricks down on top of Zindetha, practically covering the large dragon. Zindetha lay immobile on the ground.

Seeing Zindetha hit the wall and collapsing, the other meat-eating dragons took flight and started circling above Merlinius' castle.

In the clouds, Deetha had noticed that her baby, Rago, was missing. Dagger let out a mighty, thunder-like roar, calling out for his fellow family of dragons. Without waiting for them to show, Dagger and Deetha both flew off to find Rago.

Inside the castle, Odious was now advancing closer to David and Merlinius, beginning to take swipes at David with the mallet. Merlinius was still down holding his head and would have been easy to finish off if it weren't for David's bravery, who was keeping Odious at bay with his own assault. David was throwing one bottle after another at Odious, all the while darting and diving behind tables and overturned cabinets. Odious was demolishing the laboratory in his wild attempt to catch David.

Odious was totally unaware of the occurrence of the swirling pool of pulsating light which was now shooting out tendrils, lightning, and various forms of animals, monsters, and faces. This entity was by now one-fifth the size of the laboratory and was sucking in everything in its path. Finally, Odious saw the swirling vortex of colors. He stopped in his tracks, in awe of the sight.

Outside on the mountainside path, King Arturus, Jaysha, and the posse of royal knights were now arriving at the top of the mountain path. The entire posse came to an abrupt halt as they appeared from behind a bend on the mountain path. From Sir Solomon's view, he saw what appeared to be dragons circling high above Merlinius' castle.

Jaysha pointed upward, but to a different point in the sky, as she yelled, "Look, high in the clouds."

Jaysha was pointing at other dragons, the returning parents of Rago, who were coming to find their son. The two dragons flew through the clouds toward Merlinius' castle. Sir Solomon looked and noticed that there were more coming from further behind.

"Look! There are more of them! They're following the others!" Sir Solomon yelled, pointing.

"Well, what are we waiting for? Hah!" King Arturus said kicking his horse into a full gallop, leading the posse onward.

Inside Merlinius' castle, the swirling blob of brilliant colors had now engulfed nearly a fourth of the laboratory. It spun around and around as it grabbed things and pulled them into itself.

David helped Merlinius to his feet. "Are you alright?" David asked, fearing for Merlinius' safety.

As Merlinius stood and gained his balance, he saw the swirling blob of colors. "Yes lad, I'll be fine—" He stopped his speech in mid-sentence, staring in shock at the phenomenon created by the spillage of chemicals combined with the breakage of the crystal ball.

David turned and looked at the swirling thing. "What's happening?" David asked.

Merlinius replied in astonishment, "It appears that another dimension is devouring ours!"

"What did you say?" David said, puzzled.

Merlinius looked at David with great concern and tried to explain. "Listen very carefully, David. We live in a 'dimension' of time and space. A place or world that is our reality. There are other realities we cannot see…. Oh heavens! I haven't the time to teach you now!"

David stared at Merlinius, wide-eyed, as the wizard attempted to better inform him.

"The insane blob of colors that you see, David, is a gateway to another world!" Merlinius said, pointing at the swirling vortex. "Except this one is growing in a manner which I've never seen the likes of before. It appears to be swallowing up everything in its path! And that is of great danger to us David! If I don't stop this… this wild growing thing, it will destroy the world you live in! And all will disappear!"

"All? Will I disappear?" David asked.

"Yes." Merlinius nodded. At first, David stood with the look of pure fright. But then another feeling came over him, a sense of confidence, perhaps mixed with a little naiveté.

"Well, I like the way you can disappear, Merlinius!" David exclaimed. "I will help you stop this gate thing anyway I can!"

Merlinius admired the courage and bravery of David. "Thank you, Dav—" While the two temporarily ignored Odious, he prepared to make his move.

He took a giant sword off the wall and started to strike the old wizard. "Your disappearing days are over, old man!" Odious yelled.

Before Odious could strike, David charged him, giving Odious a headbutt right in the stomach, knocking the wind out of him. While Odious gasped for breath, Merlinius took advantage of his momentary lapse and seized the opportunity to look for his magical wand. In an instant, Merlinius saw and grasped his wand. With one swing of it, Merlinius sent Odious flying across the room, landing hard on the floor near the hall doorway.

In the sky above, Deman, Sadan, and the other meat-eating dragons were circling high above Merlinius' castle, like a pack of buzzards waiting to feast. From higher above them, Dagger descended, focused in on Deman.

Dagger tucked his wings and flew faster into torpedo mode. Deetha and the other plant-eating dragons followed suit. Deman was utterly blindsided by Dagger, and they both went tumbling through mid-air.

Soon after, Deetha and her crew of plant eaters collided with the other meat eaters, engaging them in a ferocious battle. Fire (lightning) was being blown, and roars (thunder) of anger were being heard throughout the world of Albion.

As the king and his posse rounded the last bend on the mountain path, they could clearly see Merlinius' castle. Up in the sky, they could also see the numerous dragons engaged in full battle.

The entire posse, from the king to knight to Jaysha, stared in total astonishment at what they were witnessing. (To us in the twenty-first century, this would be your typical lightning and thunderstorm, minus the dragons.)

Jaysha, being a devoted mother, had anxiety written all over her face. Her mother's intuition was eating her up inside. She was sure that her son's life was in certain jeopardy.

Jaysha yelled at the top of her lungs, "My son's life is in danger, we must hurry!"

This time, it was Jaysha who kicked her horse into a full gallop. The king and his posse hesitated, assessing the situation. But Sir Solomon, being the man's man that he was, forsook all concern for his own safety and kicked his horse into a full gallop.

The king and his posse then decided that there was no time to waste. They all followed Sir Solomon's cue and kicked their horses into a full gallop as well.

Jaysha hurriedly approached Merlinius' castle, with Sir Solomon and the king and posse not far behind. Up above, the battle between the meat-eating and plant-eating dragons continued to rage.

That battle was unbelievably violent. As dragon teeth sank into dragon flesh, chunks of meat were ripped entirely off a leg. Lightning bolts hit one dragon after another. To all who witnessed it, this was the battle of all battles. Down below, Rago knew that he must find his friend David. Rago took flight into a large passageway that led into the castle. He began swooping and soaring, looking everywhere for David until he finally reached the hallway leading into the laboratory.

In the laboratory, Odious, who had been knocked to the floor by the wave of Merlinius' wand, had now regained his wits and was getting up from the ground. Suddenly, as if out of nowhere, Rago came swooping in from the hallway. Odious, seeing his chance, scrambled to snare Rago's hind leg, pulling the young dragon down. David, seeing that Rago was being held, ran over and jumped onto Odious' back.

Merlinius was about to use his wand again on Odious but realized that it would be too dangerous, as David and Rago were too close and might get hurt.

David was hanging onto Odious' back, punching the villain whenever and wherever he could, while Rago was biting every chance he got. Odious was doing a pretty good job at fending off their assaults.

Then Odious saw a sharp shard of glass lying on the floor right beside him.

He bent over and grabbed it, then quickly held it to Rago's throat.

David immediately let go of Odious and yelled, "Merlinius, help!" Odious, desperate to end this tiring struggle, foolishly uttered to Merlinius, "Give me that wand and I won't slit his throat!"

"Let him go, Odious! This is between you and me!" Merlinius shouted.

Odious yelled back, "It doesn't matter who it's between old man! It's about you giving me that wand!"

David backed away, removing himself out of danger.

"You better let go of Rago! His parents will kill you!" David said. "You've got a point, kid!" Odious yelled even louder. "Give me the wand now!"

Odious began to dig the shard of glass into Rago's throat. Merlinius hesitated, but then threw the magic wand to Odious, who instantly dropped the shard of glass and caught the wand.

"There, you have what you want! Now let the dragon go!" Merlinius retorted.

Odious released Rago. "You can have the reptile, now that I have the power," he boasted.

"What does he mean, Merlinius?" David asked.

"Tell him, Merlinius. Never mind I will," said Odious. "The one who possesses the magic wand, commands the world!"

"You are mistaken, you little fool!" Merlinius responded.

"Zindetha told me your secret, old man," said Odious.

"Who's Zindetha?" David asked.

Odious smiled devilishly, "Funny you should ask, runt. Zindetha's the dragon who killed your father!"

Merlinius then put two and two together.

"You warned Zindetha that the king's royal knights were coming," said Merlinius. "That's why Zindetha was lying in wait for them that night. Sir Jonathan didn't have a chance! You've been at the bottom of this plot the whole time! You wanted the dragons all dead, and you gave King Arturus the excuse he needed! Just so you could become the king's wizard!"

A guilty smirk stole across Odious' face "Not all Dragons, I only needed a few to be my Enforcers". David meanwhile, realizing that his father's actual killer stood before him, became overwhelmed with hatred and attacked Odious in a blind rage. Caught completely off guard, Odious, with David clinging to him, went flying into tables. Odious lost his grip on the magic wand, sending it flying into the swirling vortex of colors.

"What have you done?" Merlinius screamed. "The vortex has now taken the most powerful instrument known to mankind!"

David frantically scrambled to his feet and threw whatever he could grab at Odious, eventually making his way back to where Merlinius and Rago were. The growing, swirling vortex had now grown to a third the size of the laboratory. The walls of the laboratory were starting to cave in, exposing the hallway. All kinds of things were being sucked into the swirling vortex. The vortex had not only grown larger but had also picked up speed in its rotations. Odious got back on his feet and was about to attack Merlinius, David, and Rago. He lunged toward them and was able to grab hold of David.

"You are coming with me!" Odious said, with a sinister snarl.

As Odious began dragging David away, Rago immediately started snapping, trying to bite Odious. Merlinius felt restricted from using his magical force because of his fear of hurting David. Rago, with all his might, began to roar at Odious. He roared in desperation, "Father help! Father! Father!"

"Shut up, you overgrown, wall-crawling lizard!" Odious growled as he continued dragging David along, heading toward the laboratory door. Rago continued to roar as he and Merlinius followed Odious and David out of the laboratory and into the hallway. The colorful swirling vortex had now engulfed over half the laboratory. Everything in the laboratory was getting sucked into the vortex: tables, paintings, chairs. The vortex looked like a small, but ever-growing tornado, now expanding into the hallway.

In the sky, Dagger was engaged in a firefight like no other. Suddenly, Dagger stopped in his tracks and listened. Hearing his son's call for help, Dagger soared downward bee-lining toward Merlinius' castle. Deman, whom Dagger had been fighting with, gave chase and caught up to Dagger, powerfully colliding with him. Both dragons smashed into the top of one the castles' towers. Boulders went flying everywhere as Dagger and Deman continued fighting. Meanwhile, the colorful swirling vortex was now swallowing up a large corner of Merlinius' castle.

At the mountaintop outside the castle, the king, Sir Solomon, Jaysha and the posse had all come to an abrupt halt, momentarily mesmerized by the spectacle they saw; numerous dragons fighting in mid-air, lightning strikes everywhere, and paralyzing, deafening thunder. But this bunch was the best of best, and they were on a mission.

"I know my son is in the castle! Let's go!" Jaysha said in a panic. "Wait!" Sir Solomon shouted, pointing to Merlinius' castle.

"What's that coming out from the corner!"

The swirling vortex was becoming gigantic. It was totally exploding everything apart and then sucking all the debris inside. The vortex is forever expanding with brilliant swirling colors.

"What has Merlinius done?" King Arturus asked, watching as one of the sections of Merlinius' castle was being torn apart. The king stood completely amazed at the sheer force that the swirling vortex possessed. It was literally swallowing up all in its path as it continued to grow.

"It looks like it's too late to enter the castle," stated King Arturus.

"We have to save my son!" Jaysha yelled.

"Jaysha!" shouted King Arturus. "The castle is caving in. It would be certain death for us all to go in there!"

The horses were restless as they all stared at the crumbling castle and at the battle that was raging between Dagger and Deman in such close proximity.

"I can't just sit here!" said Jaysha, once again expressing her grave concern. She was frightened now more than ever for her child. "My son is in there! My son!"

"Please, Jaysha!" King Arturus said. "Your son will not be saved if we get ourselves killed going in there now!"

In the castle hallway, Odious had David by the neck as they walked backward; meanwhile, he also kept watch on Merlinius and Rago, who were following closely. Odious finally reached a stairway in one of the castle's towers and then started walking upward. Sections of the tower were demolished from Dagger and Deman crashing into it earlier. Odious was not sure of which way to escape.

He looked back at Merlinius, very frustrated, and yelled, "Get away! I'm warning you! I'll cut his throat!" As Odious continued up the stairway, Merlinius and Rago stayed back, hesitating, hoping to appease David's captor.

From just above Merlinius' castle, Dagger was finally defeating his opponent. Deman decided to live to fight another day and made a break for it. Dagger circled Merlinius' castle, searching for Rago. Zindetha, who has been knocked out cold for quite a while, was now finally coming to. He slowly got up, gently flapped his wings a couple of times, and within seconds, was off and flying.

In the castle, Odious had reached the upper end of the tower's stairway. The rest of the tower was completely gone, and Odious' back was to the sky as he looked down the stairs at Merlinius and Rago. Merlinius, seeing Dagger flying directly above Odious, quickly closed his eyes and sent a telepathic message to Dagger.

"Dagger, see the man on top of the destroyed tower? Grab him from behind and take him away! He tried to hurt Rago and David!"

Dagger glanced down and saw Odious holding David. With the silence of a hawk, Dagger tucked in his wings and moved in for the swoop.

Merlinius saw Dagger coming in quickly and formulated a plan in his mind. Knowing that the timing had to be perfect, he waited until just the right time and then....

Merlinius yelled, "Odious, watch out!"

Merlinius' yell wasn't intended to warn, but rather to distract, Odious. As Odious turned to look, Merlinius quickly jumped up and grabbed David, just as Dagger simultaneously swooped down and grabbed Odious by the shoulders, lifting him away, leaving David in

Merlinius' arms. Seeing that Merlinius' plan had worked perfectly, Rago roared with glee.

Dagger flew away from the castle with Odious hanging from his claws. Suddenly from the side, Zindetha came and blindsided Dagger, causing Dagger to lose his grip and drop Odious.

Odious did not fall to his death but instead fell safely into the moat that surrounded Merlinius' castle. Dagger and Zindetha began fighting again in mid-air.

Odious crawled out of the moat and saw horses tied to a post. He hurriedly hobbled over and climbed onto one of the horses. Glancing around, Odious saw king Arturus and the others. He kicked his horse into a full gallop, hurrying to give the king an update.

"Merlinius is done," Odious gleefully said to himself, as he approached King Arturus and the others. "What a story I have for the king to hear."

"Is that the wizard's apprentice?" King Arturus asked Sir Solomon. Sir Solomon looked closely before answering. "Yes, that is Odious!

It was he who told us that Merlinius would betray the kingdom!"

Odious reached the king, his posse, and Jaysha. All listened to what Odious had to say.

"My lord, I said this day was coming… you can see for yourself, there is no limit to his disloyalty to you and your kingdom!" Odious paused to catch his breath. "He has a village boy hostage! I think Merlinius intends to use him as a sacrifice!"

"What!" Jaysha cried frantically when she heard Odious' story. "He's going to sacrifice a young boy?"

Without hesitation, Jaysha kicked her horse into a gallop, then kicked again and again in obvious desperation.

King Arturus shouted out orders. "Sir Solomon, you and Sir Jacob go and help Jaysha rescue her son! I and the others will stay here! I need to get some answers out of Odious."

CHAPTER 11

As Jaysha neared the castle's entrance, Sir Solomon and Sir Jacob were not far behind. The swirling vortex was now ripping into and swallowing up a full corner of Merlinius' castle. The vortex was by now at least a hundred feet high and about thirty feet in width.

King Arturus was discussing matters with the other royal knights when one of them noticed Odious galloping away.

"Hey! What do you think you're doing?" one knight yelled.

"I order you to stop!" King Arturus demanded.

Odious totally disregarded the king's command.

"He's blatantly disobeying your order, Your Majesty! What would you have me do?"

"He obviously has a death wish. Let's not join him."

King Arturus and the other knights watched as Odious rode away. Odious was clearly a man on a mission. As he rode, he said to himself, "I can't let that peasant woman save that little runt! He'll tell everyone that it was me behind everything!" Odious spurred his horse as fast as it could go toward the castle.

The tornado vortex was even more humongous now, continually growing and swallowing up everything in its path. Two dragons were fighting next to the vortex, when one of them got caught in the gravitational pull and was sucked into the vortex, completely disappearing from sight. The vortex continued to demolish Merlinius' castle.

Merlinius communicated something to Rago, then patted him on the head, and sent him off. Turning to David, Merlinius said, "Come on David! We have to hurry before it's too late."

"Why don't you just disappear?" David answered. "You know, just go and do what you do!"

"No! I can't leave you by yourself, it's too dangerous! We'll do this together!" Merlinius responded.

"I won't let you down! What did you send Rago to do?"

"You'll find out soon enough. Come on, by the look of things, we don't have much time!"

Merlinius and David headed back down the stairway and then down one of the many hallways in Merlinius' castle.

Jaysha jumped off her horse just as the two knights ordered to help her finally caught up. Jaysha, Sir Solomon, and Sir Jacob immediately entered the castle. A few moments later, Odious rode up and dismounted very quietly. Odious proceeded cautiously, wanting to keep his presence a secret from Jaysha and the two knights. Jaysha ran down the hallways of the castle calling for her son.

"David, where are you? David! David!" Jaysha desperately screamed.

Jaysha looked through ripped apart doors, crumbled walls, and demolished rooms. Suddenly, a gust of wind blew her off her feet. The vortex had accelerated and grown so huge that it was now taller than Merlinius' castle, twisting and turning without any certain path or direction.

Jaysha could see that Merlinious' laboratory was in ruins. The vortex was bigger than ever and was only about forty feet away from her. The gravitational pull had Jaysha in an almost horizontal position.

She hung onto a pillar for dear life, as Sir Solomon and the other knight desperately tried to reach her and pull her to safety. Just when Jaysha was about to give up and let go, the twisting, turning vortex shifted and whirled in the opposite direction. Jaysha fell to the ground, and Sir Solomon swiftly swept her into his arms and out of danger.

Rago was flying above when he suddenly stalled in mid-air, his ears twitching and standing on end. Rago quickly turned back around and soared down in the direction of the laboratory. Rago came flying down and saw David's mother standing, but still leaning on Sir Solomon. Rago then glided over to Jaysha, who was still mesmerized by the monstrous tornado.

From within the laboratory, the swirling vortex was now moving away in a sharp, zigzagging manner. Jaysha, dazed, was being attended to by the two royal knights and did not realize that Rago was about to land right in front of her.

Sir Solomon, seeing the baby dragon, immediately took his bow and loaded an arrow. He raised the arrow and took aim, ready to fire.

"I'll kill you, demon!"

Jaysha looked as Sir Solomon pointed the arrow directly at the small dragon. Jaysha took a closer look and then recognized the young dragon. "Rago ?" Jaysha leaped up to try to stop the killing.

"Get out of the way!!" Sir Solomon yelled.

Jaysha swung back around to face Sir Solomon. The knight let the arrow fly.

"No-no-no-oo!!" Jaysha shouted.

Without thinking, Jaysha stuck her hand directly, in the path of the arrow, catching it in mid-air. Jaysha turned and gave Rago a big smile.

"This dragon is the Dragons my Son told me about, He's my son's friend!" she told Sir Solomon. "Maybe he can help us. We need to find my son and the wizard!"

Jaysha tried to communicate with Rago, using the sign language which she had seen David use.

"Where is my son, David? Does Merlinius have him captive somewhere here in the castle?"

Rago looked at her, puzzled. Rago then looked at the stairway.

Jaysha was trying hard to understand what Rago was telling her.

A loud humming sound, like that of a howling wind tunnel, could suddenly be heard in the background. Everyone stopped to look out of the opening made by the crumbled walls of the lab. The sound was made by the swirling vortex, which had again changed direction and was coming back towards the lab. Jaysha's eyes focused on the vortex, which was fast coming toward her. Rago took off flying and snagged Jaysha's clothing, pulling her to follow.

Rago flew toward the stairway and stalled, waiting long enough to make sure that Jaysha was right behind him, which she was.

The two knights were by now exasperated by the entire debacle. Still, they immediately followed Jaysha, without a clue that Odious was only twenty paces behind them. Odious, very cautious not to be seen trailing them, saw a broken off piece of steel rod and picked it up. "Just what I needed!" Odious said to himself, continuing after Jaysha and the knights.

Merlinius and David approached a section of the stairway that had collapsed. Merlinius, without hesitation, magically appeared on the other side. He motioned back for David to jump, which the brave lad did immediately, making it look simple. However, as he landed, a piece of the stairway crumbled underneath him, causing him to lose his balance and begin to fall. David grabbed hold and held on for dear life.

"Oh no!" David shouted. "Help! Merlinius, help!"

Merlinius quickly threw David a rope which he seemed to conjure out of thin air. David held on tight as the magician pulled him to safety.

"Good job, my lad!" exclaimed the impressed wizard.

Merlinius discarded the rope, and both of them continued at a fast pace up the stairway, arriving quickly at the top.

David, exhausted from the climb, sat back against the wall. Merlinius, on the other hand, knew that he had no time to rest.

He went over to a glass case which contained a crystal ball with the same radiant colors as those of the swirling vortex. Merlinius carefully picked it up and carried it out onto the balcony of the castle tower.

Once outside, Merlinius looked over the castle and its grounds. He was aghast as he surveyed the devastation, which he knew was at least in part caused by his great idea to give the dragons the magic spell of weightlessness. But inside, he knew that if he had the whole thing to do over, he would probably do it again.

"See what happens when you play god?" Merlinius chided himself. "Destruction!" Merlinius gathered himself and frantically looked all over for Rago.

"Rago, you're supposed to be here waiting! I need you!"

Rago was nowhere in sight. David came out to see if he could help. "Don't worry, Rago will show up! I promise!"

"I need to get this crystal ball into the center of that vortex!" said Merlinius. "Without my wand, I can't use the electromagnetic property that powers my wishes! We need Rago to fly and carry this crystal ball to the top of the vortex and then drop it into its center!"

Merlinius turned to look at the swirling vortex which was now bigger than ever . He wondered if it might be too late.

Inside, Jaysha and the two knights were still following Rago. They finally reached the collapsed section of the stairway where Merlinius and David had experienced trouble crossing earlier.

Rago was floating, waiting for Jaysha. But after a few moments, it became apparent that Jaysha wasn't just going to leap over. Rago decided not to wait, sensing that Merlinius needed him now.

"Have to go now! Bye!" Rago Roared.

Jaysha watched Rago fly away. "Wait, where's David?" Feeling the urgency, Jaysha yelled back to the knights…

"I'm jumping! I'll throw that rope over to you when I get across!" Jaysha said as she pointed to the rope that David and Merlinius had used earlier.

"Alright! We'll be right behind you!" Sir Solomon said, turning to the other knight, Sir Jacob. "I'll go first."

Sir Jacob nodded in agreement. Jaysha then prepared to jump. "One, two and thre—ee!"

Jaysha jumped and grabbed on to the stairway, which then collapsed. She started to free fall but then, with cat-like reflexes, she caught on to the rope. The knights watched in panic and wanted to help, but she was too far out of their reach.

After some struggle, Jaysha climbed the rope and finally reached the top on the other side. She looked toward the two knights, and behind them, she could see Odious, who had earlier told her about her son. At first, she smiled, thinking he was going to give assistance, until…

Odious, who was now right behind Sir Jacob, lifted up and swung the steel rod at Sir Jacob. The poor knight did not even know what hit him. Sir Jacob screamed in pain and fell off the stairs to his death.

Odious then took a swing at Sir Solomon, who immediately began to fight back quite valiantly. Jaysha could see that Sir Solomon was in trouble. She quickly pulled out a knife and waited for a clear throw as the two men moved in and out of each other's way.

Finally, Jaysha saw her chance and threw a direct hit. The knife stuck deep into Odious' chest, and the fight came to an abrupt halt. Sir Solomon looked at the severely wounded Odious, thinking that he was a dead man.

Odious looked down and saw the knife planted firmly within his chest. "Nicely done," he said, yanking the knife out of his chest. "But to kill a wizard, you have to…" He paused before turning to plunge Jaysha's knife directly into Sir Solomon's chest. Jaysha looked on in horror as Odious finished his statement, "…destroy his brain!"

Sir Solomon, with Jaysha's knife stuck in his chest, fell off the stairway.

Odious' chest wound was rapidly healing and within seconds was entirely gone. Jaysha stared at Odious in utter confusion. Odious looked at her like a hungry tiger.

"If only I had been able to kill your brat! We could've avoided all this!" Odious used his mage to throw the steel rod point-blank at Jaysha. But, amazingly enough,

just like the arrow, Jaysha caught the steel rod in midair and then smiled at Odious.

"I don't know who you are, but I do know… you deserve this!" Jaysha threw the steel rod swiftly and forcefully, sticking Odious directly through his forehead. Odious stumbled and staggered as he tried to pull out the steel rod from his skull. "Thanks for telling me where to aim! Fool!"

Odious' lifeless body toppled down the center of the tower. Jaysha looked up the stairway. "David!" she called.

Jaysha continued climbing the stairway in hopes of finding her son.

King Arturus and the royal knights were getting very impatient waiting for Odious, the knights and Jaysha to return. King Arturus looked at Merlinius' castle in ruins.

"I'm afraid we may have lost them all!" King Arturus despaired. "My king! Sir Solomon is your best knight!" howled one of the knights, despondently. "They will return soon! I'm sure of it!" "Well, let's hope you're right!" said King Arturus.

"I must request your retreat to safer ground," continued the knight. "For the sake of the kingdom! I will take two other men and go and look for them!"

"What! And lose three more?" questioned King Arturus.

The king and his men took their eyes off the swirling vortex during their conversation. The vortex which had been at some distance from them was now turning and coming towards the king and his men.

The rampaging tornado raced toward the group of men. A knight felt the wind picking up and looked toward the group.

"The wind storm is too strong! Retreat!… Retreat!"

The king hastily mounted and galloped away safely. But half of the posse of royal knights were not so lucky. They, along with their horses, were suddenly sucked into the swirling vortex and vanished from existence.

CHAPTER 12

Merlinius and David were still waiting for the appearance of Rago. Merlinius' face displayed a defeated look when suddenly he heard David's voice ring out, "There he is!"

Rago appeared flying out from behind the walls of what was left of the castle's north side. Pure joy burst on the faces of Merlinius and David as they saw Rago flying toward them.

However, seemingly out of nowhere, Deman came soaring toward Rago. Before Deman could reach the small dragon, Deetha came flying in from the side and cut off Deman. Both dragons started to engage in a ferocious battle. Rago watched his mother fighting fiercely, when suddenly the swirling vortex came into the picture, threatening to devour both dragons. Rago panicked and he started to fly over to warn his mother. But before he could do so, the vortex tornado sucked in both Deetha and Deman. Rago watches shocked as his mother vanished, then turned and swiftly flew toward Merlinius.

Merlinius was still clutching the crystal ball which provided the only hope of stopping the vortex. Rago flew up to Merlinius and landed right next to him.

"Rago you must fly to the top and go directly to the center of it! You must then drop the crystal ball directly into it."

Merlinius handed the crystal ball to Rago, who leaned back onto his tail and then took the ball with his front legs and hands. Rago looked at David, who smiled.

"I'm so sorry about your mom! Maybe we can save her and the others? Time for you to be the hero, buddy!"

Rago attempted to smile back, though it is very hard for a dragon to smile.

Rago then took off, up and away, toward the vortex.

David and Merlinius watched together the spectacle of the vortex, which had expanded high above the castle and was now turning toward the castle's central tower. This was the exact location of David and Merlinius. Merlinius began backing up, shouting at David, "Run back down the stairs! Fast!"

David and Merlinius barely made it back inside the tower before the vortex ripped into the corner of the tower, causing an earthquake effect. Multiple bricks and stones tumbled and fell. The wizard and the boy were both knocked to the floor by the impact.

The impact also knocked Jaysha off the stairs, but miraculously, she was able to grab hold of an iron rod protruding from the wall. As she dangled, Jaysha could see that the floor below was easily over a hundred feet down. The swirling vortex again changed its direction, leaving the tower partially demolished. David and Merlinius came back out onto the tower balcony, both in awe of the event.

The enormous vortex of brilliant colors moved in the direction of some dragons which were still battling, but they were too busy fighting to realize that they needed to be running to escape. Thus, they were pulled in by the gravitational force of the vortex power.

Zindetha and Dagger were pulled into the vortex together, both dragons perishing.

Rago moved closer to the top of the swirling vortex, all the while struggling to keep from being pulled in himself. With all his might,

Rago fought to reach the top but was gradually losing more and more strength in his wings.

The swirling vortex, now even larger than it was when it hit the tower just moments ago, again changed directions and headed back toward Merlinius' castle.

Rago appeared ready to give up, as he lacked the power to resist the pull of the vortex any longer. However, his ears caught the sound of David's mother calling out for her son, causing him to dig deep down until he somehow found the inner strength to press on.

David was thrilled to hear his mother's voice calling out for him. "Mom, I'm here!" he shouted, running to find her. "Mom! Where are you?"

Rago somehow reached the top center of the vortex. Looking down at its center, he could not believe what he saw. The center consisted of a pitch black hole, which appeared to be endless. A wall of various colors radiated brilliantly as it swirled, encircling the black center.

The journey to the top proved too much for Rago. With absolutely no strength left, Rago fell, still clutching the crystal ball, into the center of the swirling vortex. As he fell, he said to himself, "At least I can die with my family." Both Rago and the crystal ball vanished into the center of the vortex. Within moments, a tremendous explosion occurred. A blinding white light shot straight out of the vortex in a flat wave. This was followed by another explosion, creating a ball of electricity which expanded a thousand times the size of a crystal ball. The massive ball of electricity quickly constricted into a colored ball of light no bigger than a baseball, and then slowly faded from sight.

In the aftermath, everything that had vanished into the swirling vortex during its existence remained missing. About half of Merlinius' vast castle remained.

David finally found his mother, barely able to stand on her feet, on the stairway next to the partially blown apart tower wall. David looked at his mother with tremendous relief. Both embraced, then Jaysha pulled back partially, but still held on to her son.

"You're grounded, young man!"

"Mom, my friend saved us! Rago saved us all!"

"Did he, honey?"

"Yes mom, he did! He's with his family now… I hope."

Merlinius interrupted the tender and sad moment, "I think we should get out of here before we are all lost under a pile of rocks!"

"Yes" shouted Jaysha. "Let's get outta here!"

David, Merlinius, and Jaysha began slowly walking down the mostly demolished stairwell. David looked up at Merlinius. "Rago's gone, isn't he?"

"Well, I think he went to be with his family."

"Went to be with his family? Where?" David questioned Merlinius. Merlinius explained, "Can't say for sure. Perhaps another world. Perhaps another dimension? I wish I could have gone in myself, just to see it!" As Merlinius, David and Jaysha climbed down the stairwell, they could see Sir Solomon at the bottom, lying dead with the knife still in his chest.

Jaysha looked with sadness at Sir Solomon's lifeless body. As tears gathered in her eyes, she wiped them away. Merlinius looked down at the slain knight, then back to tearful Jaysha.

"Maybe even without my wand, I can still work some magic?" Merlinius said.

Merlinius went over and knelt next to Sir Solomon. He carefully removed the knife out of Sir Solomon's chest. Jaysha and David both winced in reaction to Merlinius' actions. They then turned to each other with hopeful looks on their faces.

Merlinius threw the knife to the side and then calmly reflexed his shoulders. He then bowed his head and closed his eyes. As seconds ticked by, Merlinius stretched his arms out above Sir Solomon's body and then started to move his hands, with palms down, back and forth across the dead knight's chest.

Merlinius began mumbling and whispering ancient Latin words.

"The powers from the stars that giveth… has been taken away.… Through me, I pass life… for his to return… unto him! From the stars that giveth life for eternity."

Before Merlinius could even finish speaking, the healing transformation of Sir Solomon's wound had already begun. The open puncture was growing back, and skin was closing. The knife wound completely healed, and soon after, Sir Solomon's eyes blinked open. He immediately began to moan and groan. Jaysha's joy expressed itself in loud laughter, which spread to both Merlinius and David. Sir Solomon slowly sat up, confused with the notion that he was being laughed at.

"Has everyone lost their minds?" Sir Solomon asked. "What's so funny?" They continued to laugh, but even a little louder.

Together, Merlinius, David, Jaysha and Sir Solomon walked away from the demolished castle. King Arturus and the remaining royal knights waited to meet them.

David was feeling very sad about losing his friend, Rago. "Merlinius, so you really don't know where the dragons have gone?" David softly asked. "Do you think Rago died?"

"David, the crystal ball Rago took with him into the center of the vortex was an astral dimension," Merlinius explained. "It reaches beyond the stars, without borders, without boundaries."

"Astral dimension? I don't understand." David looked even more confused than before.

"Infinity David, without limits, forever and ever, never-ending!" Merlinius said, putting a tender hand on David's shoulder.

"Look up, David," said Merlinius. Both of them looked upward. "Beyond the sky, there is space, which goes on forever and ever! David, there is no end!"

"And that's where the vortex is!" Merlinius exclaimed, pointing to the sky. "Gone, up there forever!"

"So, Rago is gone forever?" David asked.

Merlinius did not answer. Then suddenly, all of them saw lightning and then heard thunder in the distant clouds. Merlinius groaned in frustration and then responded.

"Oh no! Their sound waves and atmospheric electron properties still exist! Only the physical matter of the dragons has vanished!"

"Rago isn't gone!" David asked excitedly.

Merlinius gave David a surprising look.

"I can see I have so much to teach you, my boy," Merlinius said. "How would you like to work for an old, crotchety wizard? The pay is little, the company sometimes wretched, but you will learn all I know." David looked at the wizard a bit puzzled. Then, he understood. He looked up to his mother Jaysha and Sir Solomon. They both nodded 'yes.'

Reilly's House Ray Evans sat near the fireplace, having finished the story. He noticed that his little sweetheart, Reilly, had fallen asleep on his lap during the telling of the story of Rago. He looked at her for a moment and then said with a big smile, "You've fallen asleep hugging your little dragon friend."

Suddenly, with his peripheral vision, Mr. Evans thought he saw the toy dragon move. He looked twice at the toy dragon, thinking that he saw its eyes blink. Mr. Evans shook his head in disbelief as he picked up the dragon, surveying it from every angle.

"Hmm, I must be tired and my mind's playing tricks on me," he whispered to himself. "Or maybe it was just shadows from the fire?" He placed the toy back into the girl's hands, gently got up and carried little Reilly to her bedroom.

Reilly's father laid his daughter down and tucked her into bed. He slowly removed the toy dragon from her clutching hands. The little girl moaned and said softly, "Rago… don't fly away.…"

Mr. Evans then placed the toy dragon on her dresser. As he left the room, he stopped at the doorway and glanced back at the dragon toy, a smirk curling his lips.

"What a kook that old man was… talking to a toy and insisting that he was the infamous Merlinius!" said,

Mr. Evans, as he closed his daughter's bedroom door. "Still, I can't believe he gave me his treasure for free! 'Give the little dragon plenty of water,' he says! Yeah right!" Mr. Evans walked down the hall chuckling to himself.

Mr. Evans went to the kitchen to fix some coffee. He smiled as he said to himself while stirring his coffee, "Jet lag! These trips are getting too long… I swear I saw that toy dragon move! I need to get to bed!" Mr. Evans climbed into bed and pillowed his head which was still spinning with confusion at what he thought he may have seen. "It couldn't be," he muttered again as he tried to still his thoughts. As he began to drift off to sleep, his mind flashed back to when he had bought the toy dragon.

Ray Evans waved goodbye to the old man standing behind the counter. The old man smiled and waved back as Mr. Evans walked toward the door. He shook his head briefly before proceeding outside. As he did the old man emerged from behind the counter smiling ever so slightly to himself… and disappeared. Though Mr. Evans wasn't aware of it, he had just encountered Merlinius wearing modern clothes.

Merlinius appeared out of thin air in front of David's house and knocked very lightly at the door. David, who was expecting Merlinius, quietly opened the door and snuck out.

"Did you find him a good home? David anxiously inquired. "Please tell me you did!"

Merlinius replied joyfully, "Yes, yes, my friend."

"Where is he? Merlinius?" David asked impatiently.

"He's with a little girl who just adores him!"

"He's doing fine then?" David asked.

"Yes, and don't worry David. I almost have the answer as to how to bring Rago back!"

"I'm not worried," David said, smiling as he looked up into the stars.

"It's harder than I thought," said Merlinius. "It's not that easy for me to go from one dimension to another without my magic wand!"

"You're a wizard!" David laughed. "You'll figure out how to do it."

Reilly slept peacefully as across the room, on top of her dresser, the toy dragon, Rago, began to move, fantastically coming to life. Rago flapped his wings and blurted out a tiny roar.

"It's tough, after being unable to move for so long!" the toy dragon complained before looking at Reilly as she slept. "She looks like she can keep a secret." Holding the crystal ball, Rago flew around the room.

"This looks like a friendly place," Rago muttered to himself as he looked around.

Rago inspected Reilly's collection of various kinds of stuffed toy dragons. He flew toward a window as if to go through it, then slammed into it and bounced off of the glass. After bouncing off the window, Rago stared at it in amazement.

"Wow! They have walls you can see through!" he exclaimed.

Rago looked out of the window at the city beyond. "Look at all those torches! Too many to count!"

Then he closed his eyes and sent his old wizard friend a telepathic message: "Merlinius, please find a way to get me back home."

9 798893 895650